Bed of Roses

Sharon Hendryx McDaniel

PublishAmerica
Baltimore

ISBN: 1-4241-8239-5
PUBLISHED BY PUBLISHAMERICA, LLLP
www.publishamerica.com
Baltimore

Printed in the United States of America

Prologue

Kayla Price stood at the top of the hill that she had just climbed. Looking down to see the roof of her house, she became slightly dizzy.

"Why in the world am I doing this?" she asked herself.

Of course she knew why she had climbed the hill; she was searching for rocks that she could use to border yet another flower bed that she was going to make, a rose garden. For the past few weeks she had been planning to do this, now she just had to keep her mind set on the task.

She was finding it hard these days to keep her mind on anything other than the recent breakup with her boyfriend; it came on the heels of her father's death—well not exactly.

Her father had passed away a few months earlier, but to Kayla it seemed like only yesterday...when out of the blue Steve had dumped her.

It wasn't as if she were in love with Steve, but he had been good company, someone who had always been there when she needed a friend. At that very moment Kayla realized that's all that Steve had been, her friend. It wasn't fair of her to be mad at him for leaving at a time when she needed him most. He deserved to have his own life.

As she gathered up rocks she put them in a pile. She had

planned to return to the top of the hill the next morning with her four wheeler to haul them down with.

Just as she was about to call it a day she spotted one more rock, it stood tall and was covered thickly with green moss, it reminded Kayla of a waterfall, the way the moss cascaded over the rock, she knew that it would be the perfect centerpiece for her new rose garden.

As Kayla walked closer to the rock she could see that it had something carved into it, she ran her fingers across the deep grooves of the writing. It spelled out the letters *KIN*.

As she spoke the letters out loud suddenly she felt a tingling sensation, a mild shock, she pulled her hand back and let it dangle limply at her side, she wasn't sure how long she had been standing there in a trance but a voice pulled her attention away from the rock, someone was calling her name.

Kayla walked to the edge of the hill and looked over, there she saw her chubby friend Shelly looking up at her with wild eyes, she was on her knees struggling to catch her breath. The woman had always been such a drama queen, Kayla thought.

"What on God's green earth are you doing up there?" Shelly asked.

"Getting some much-needed exercise, come on up," Kayla invited.

Shelly gave her friend a look that clearly let her know that she was not happy to be there.

"Why don't you come down?"

Kayla smiled and slowly jogged down the hill to where her friend stood.

"So what brings you here?" Kayla asked.

"Well, we haven't had a girls day in a while so I thought we could go for pizza."

"The last thing I need is pizza," she told Shelly, remembering the trouble she had getting to the top of that hill only an hour or so earlier. Kayla was not overweight by any means, but she was a little out of shape, she just hadn't had the mental strength lately to keep up with anything, she missed her parents dearly.

"Okay, see you later." Shelly turned and started to walk away.

"Wait up, I didn't say no, I just said I didn't need it."

"Well, neither of us really need to eat pizza, but have we ever let that stop us before?"

"Never." They giggled in unison.

"So what did you say that you were doing up there?" Shelly asked, looking back to the hilltop.

"I was looking for rocks to border my new rose bed."

"I can't believe that you are making another flower bed, do you ever stop? Don't answer that," she said, holding her hand in the air. "I can tell you that there are plenty of rocks down here, you didn't have to climb that hill." Shelly made a sweeping motion with her arms to the ground in front of them.

Kayla bent down to retrieve one of the rocks that Shelly had been referring to. She studied it closely for a moment before she tossed it at her best friend's feet. "This is not a rock, it is a pebble."

"Ouch!" Shelly winced as if it had really hurt.

"Sorry."

"Well, whatever you want to call them, it makes no difference to me, if you want to waste your time go right ahead, did you find anything up there besides rocks?"

"Like what?"

"I don't know, buried treasure, anything."

"Well, since you asked, I did find a beautiful rock that would make a perfect centerpiece, but..." She hesitated.

"But what?"

"Well, it's kind of strange."

Shelly rolled her eyes at her friend. "What could be so strange about a rock?" Rocks were all the same to Shelly, but she would listen to her friend because this particular rock seemed to intrigue her.

"First of all, it has the letters *KIN* carved into it, and when I touched it… Well, let's just say I got a strange feeling."

"That feeling you got was simply a dizzy sensation brought on by the high altitude and the climb of that steep hill."

Kayla ignored her remark. "What if that is someone's grave?" Kayla asked. "What if some one is really buried under that rock?"

"Don't be ridiculous, I'm sure some kid just carved his name in that rock, some kid that can't spell his name right, nonetheless just some kid…and even if some one is buried under that rock, what can a dead man do to you?"

Kayla thought for a moment. "Yeah , you're right. What can a dead man do to me?"

As she spoke the words she felt a rush of cold air and goose bumps cover her entire body.

ONE

Present time

Kayla Price sighed as she dropped to her knees, landing in the flowerbed located just outside of her bedroom window.

She began to pull dead leaves from her prize-winning rose bushes, paying no attention to the thorns that pierced her delicate skin, or the blood droplets that now stained the legs of her jeans.

In her mind, Kayla had been reliving the moment when Steve Williams, her boyfriend of two years, had suddenly out of nowhere told her that it was over between them. Okay, so it had happened four months ago and she thought she had gotten over it, she hadn't thought much about Steve until that very morning when she went to the mailbox and pulled out a wedding invitation to Steve and Melissa's wedding.

She could not believe it, they had only been seeing each other for a few months, and now she had him in her clutches, the little princess; all she was good for was spending her Daddy's money.

Kayla looked down to see her flesh wounds, but they were not what bothered her; what bothered her was that Steve really loved this girl, she could see it in his eyes, when she bumped into him at the grocery store two weeks earlier he was beaming, she never saw that look in his eyes when they were together, he

9

loved Melissa and Kayla had never been more than a friend to him. Yes, Steve had found someone to spend his life with and she still had no one. All she had to hold on to was the strange man who appeared to her in her dreams almost on a nightly basis , I guess you could say that he was the man of her dreams, but every time this man showed up his face always seemed to be hidden in the shadows. But Kayla knew that he would be remarkable, she had always told herself that when the right man came along it would not matter what he looked like but what was on the inside was what matters, but let's face it, it wouldn't hurt her feelings if the man she fell in love with turned out to be drop-dead gorgeous.

"Who are you kidding, Kayla? You're thirty-something years old and when you turn sixty you will still be sitting here alone in the same old flowerbed picking dead leaves off of the same old rose bushes," she told herself, tossing her gardening gloves into the air, not caring where they landed; after all, they hadn't protected her from the thorns anyway. She wiped her bloody hands on her jeans.

"Excuse me, I didn't mean to interrupt the conversation you seem to be having with yourself, but I—"

Kayla let out a yelp. She was startled by the voice and she turned to face the owner of it.

"Jake, I didn't hear you drive up." She wiped some of the loose dirt from her clothing and pulled a long, curly red lock of hair from her face, tucking it securely behind her ear.

"I didn't drive, I walked. And it doesn't surprise me that you didn't hear me approaching; after all, you were talking to your self rather loudly."

Jake tried not to notice how incredibly sexy she looked this morning. She brushed the hair out of her face again, making a path for a bead of sweat to run from her forehead down her slightly freckled cheek, off her chin to land in the crevasse between her ample breasts.

"I was not talking to myself," she denied stubbornly.

"Oh really." Jake crossed his arms over his chest and smiled at her in amusement. It was not the first time that he had caught her talking to herself and every time she denied it.

"All right, I was talking to myself, but it's not like I do it all the time; I'm just not feeling myself today."

"When are you going to forget about that guy Steve and go out with me?"

"Jake, I've told you before that we shouldn't go out, we work together. We are friends and I just don't want to ruin that."

Jake rolled his eyes, he had heard all of this before and it still infuriated him. He had a thing for this woman and she just would not let it happen. Maybe it wouldn't lead anywhere but the least she could do was try, let him have a chance to show her how good they could be together, he was sure they would remain friends even if a romance didn't work out, he just had to convince her of this.

"You know what your problem is, Kayla?"

"No, but I am sure that you are going to tell me, Jake." Kayla looked up at the sky, acting like a child that was about to be scolded.

Jake was about to let her have it, he was going to lay it out on the table for her, but at the last minute he changed his mind, he would just be wasting his breath anyway. "Actually, I think I'll just keep my mouth shut and let you figure this one out for yourself."

Kayla put a hand on her chest and gasped in surprise. "Jake, keeping his mouth shut, that's a first... By the way, was there something that you wanted or did you just come over to point out my weaknesses?"

Jake didn't want to point out her weaknesses and he didn't want to make her feel bad either; what he did want to do was take her by the shoulders, pull her close and give her the longest, deepest kiss that any man had ever given her. He thought better.

"I need some materials to fix the fence on the west side of the property," he finally spit out.

"I didn't know the fence was broken , why didn't you tell me sooner?"

"I just found out myself. I pinned the cattle up on top of the hill until I can get it fixed."

"Did we lose any cattle?"

"About fifty head, as far as I can tell."

Kayla sighed, this wasn't the first time that they had lost cattle and had to mend broken fences; she had a gut feeling it wouldn't be the last either.

"I'll get the checkbook." As she walked towards the old ranch house she didn't remember her father having so much trouble with the ranch when he was alive.

"Thanks, babe," Jake told her as he followed behind her.

"Don't call me babe," she said over her shoulder.

Kayla walked into the parlor of the house and opened up the drawer of the old desk where her father always sat to write out the bills every month. He always kept a little stash of what he called rainy day cash. Kayla remembered when she was young, her father would call her in from playing outside on a hot summer day, the conversation was always the same.

"Didn't you notice the clouds building up outside today?" he would ask.

"Daddy, there is not a cloud in the sky," she would tell him.

"Oh but there is, I see rain clouds, Kay Kay, and you know what that means."

"It's gonna rain?" she asked, confused.

"Yes, and that means we get to use some of our rainy day money."

"What are we gonna spend it on, Daddy?"

"Well, since we can't do anything outside in the rain I guess we just have to go to the ice cream parlor, we can watch the rain from the window while we have ice cream."

"That's a wonderful idea, Daddy."

Kayla could remember clearly, she would get one scoop of vanilla and one scoop of chocolate and her father would always get a root beer float, her Mamma used to say good thing root beer didn't have alcohol in it or Daddy would be a drunk. He sure did like that stuff. She remembered fondly.

Once they had made their purchase they would sit in front of the picture window and pretend to watch the rain, people would look at them like they were crazy but it didn't bother them at all, they were in their own world when they were at the ice cream parlor.

This ritual between her and her father started when she was just six years old and every summer at least once a week her father would take her for ice cream. It was Kayla's thirty-sixth birthday when they sat together in the ice cream parlor for the last time , they stared out the window together as they always did, but she knew that there was something very different about this trip, she could hear a difference in his voice and she could see the sadness in his eyes.

"I love you, Kay Kay."

"I love you too, Daddy."

It would be the very last time she would get to tell him that because that very night her father died in his sleep, the doctors said he had a heart attack, Kayla knew that he died from a broken heart, he had been so lonely without her mother, who had passed away six months earlier.

Kayla shook herself from the past and returned to the present. She handed Jake a blank check.

"Thanks, babe." Jake saw the tear that escaped from the corner of her eye. He knew not to ask any questions, he was sure that she was thinking of her dad; he'd only been gone for a few months, the pain was still fresh for her and even for him. Jake had only worked for the man for six years but in those years they had become close, he was like a father to Jake also.

"I said don't call me babe." She really didn't mind that he called her that but she didn't want him to know that.

Kayla stood at the front porch and watched Jake walk down the driveway, even she could not deny the fact that Jake was a very nice-looking man, he was tall and slender, but strong, he had jet-black hair and dark brown eyes , he even had a thin mustache. Kayla usually didn't like a mustache on a man but it suited Jake well. She remembered the first day he came to work for her dad, six years ago, it seemed like yesterday, time had gone by so fast. Kayla's father trusted Jake with his farm and his family so it was no surprise when he asked Jake to continue on at the ranch even after he was gone. Jake promised to take care of the ranch and of Kayla.

So far it had been a good thing, Jake took care of everything but the finances, that was Kayla's job.

Kayla turned her attention back to her rose bushes and that was when she noticed the large footprints in the dirt directly under her bedroom window; by the size of the prints, they obviously belonged to a man...a big man, she thought.

Kayla got a sick feeling in the pit of her stomach, she jumped up and ran to the edge of the driveway screaming for Jake to come back.

He ran back up the drive as fast as he could, when he reached her he looked her up and down, he didn't see any blood gushing from her head, or anywhere else for that matter; she didn't look physically hurt.

"What the hell are you screaming about?" he asked almost in annoyance.

"Have you been walking in my flowerbed?" she demanded to know.

"No, you'd have my hide if I did that."

"Someone has been in it." She pointed at the footprints.

It was obvious to Jake that the prints were very fresh. He didn't like the fact that someone had been at her window, possibly watching her.

"It wasn't me, but I will check around, it could have been one of the ranch hands." It had better not have been one of his men, he had warned them all to stay clear of her. If they knew what was good for them they would obey his warnings.

"Why would they be down by the house?"

"Maybe they just wanted to sneak a peek at the boss lady." He tried to lighten the mood; he didn't want her to be scared.

"I don't think it's funny, Jake."

The smile left Jake's face. "All right. I'll look into it and make sure my men know not to be around the house unless they are with me."

"Thank you, Jake." He was probably right, it may have just been one of the ranch hands, but whoever it was had been right by her window, they could have seen her changing, or watched her while she slept. It gave her the chills to think that someone might had been watching her every move.

"I'm only at the end of the driveway if you need me," he told her. "But if you're scared I could stay the night," he offered.

"I'm sure you would, but I think that I will be fine."

"All right, just call me if you need me." He gave her shoulder a reassuring squeeze.

"I will," she promised. Kayla stretched her arms over her head and took a deep breath. It smelled like rain; it would be summer soon and if she wanted to build that new rose bed she would have to get busy before it got too hot; she had already decided that she wanted to border the new bed with large rocks and to do that she would have to climb the steep hill behind the house. She was half tempted to ask Jake to help her but thought better of it; he had enough to take care of without having to help her haul rocks around. She would just do it herself, but for the moment she would focus on shaping up the existing flowerbeds.

Kayla had been working for hours without taking a break. When she finally stopped to look up she noticed the storm clouds overhead.

"Typical Oklahoma weather, you never know what's coming until it gets here and bites you in the butt," she told herself.

She walked around to the front porch and poured herself a

glass of lemonade. As she sipped, the rain came down, slowly at first, then harder. Suddenly the wind picked up. It sounded like a freight train was about to come through the front yard.

She hadn't heard Jake until he stood directly in front of her, arms flailing about.

"What's the matter?"

"There's a twister coming, get your pretty little ass into the cellar...NOW!" he ordered.

"I didn't hear any warnings."

"I'm warning you." He pointed to the west, where Kayla could see a funnel cloud approaching them, and it was coming fast.

Kayla willed her feet to move but they wouldn't. She had heard stories of twisters when she was growing up but she had never experienced one herself. She stood in awe of this work of nature, the rain came faster and harder and then the hail, it was huge, and it hurt.

Jake came up behind her and scooped her into his arms, the hail pelting their bodies as he struggled to open the cellar door. He carried her down the steep stairway, the wind slammed the door shut behind them. Kayla started to shake, Jake tried to hold her in his arms. He wanted to comfort her, but she wouldn't let him. She pulled away and retreated to a corner like a scared little animal.

They sat in the darkness of the cellar and listened while the wind played havoc with the lawn furniture overhead.

"Is the house going to be destroyed?" she asked Jake.

She couldn't lose the house, she just couldn't, it was all she had left of her parents, there were so many wonderful memories in that house.

"It would have to take a direct hit to tear that house apart, I don't think you have anything to worry about." He pulled her wet, shivering body closer to him. He hoped the storm would not take the house.

"You're so cold," he told her.

"I'm fine," she insisted, trying to escape his hold.

"Don't lie to me." He held her tighter so that she could not escape his grip this time.

"Why can't you just let someone take care of you? What are you so scared about?"

Kayla felt as if she needed to defend herself. "I am not scared, Jake. I am not afraid to let anyone care about me, you just think that you know it all; well, let me tell you something, you don't know it all, and you don't know me."

"I never claimed to know it all, but like it or not, I do know you."

"I don't want to talk anymore." She folded her arms across her chest and turned her back to him.

"Maybe you should talk about it, it might do you some good to talk to someone beside yourself."

Oh boy! He had done it now. Kayla turned red from embarrassment or possibly anger. "I told you, that's not a habit," she snapped at him.

"And I told you—"

Before he could finish there was a loud banging on the cellar door. "Boss, are you in there?"

"Who is that?" Kayla asked. She didn't recognize the voice.

"It's Matt, he's a new hand, hired him about a month ago."

Jake and Kayla climbed out of the cellar and looked around. The house appeared to be in one piece, except for a few shingles missing from the roof. The rain had stopped and the sky was clear once again.

"It must have went right over us," Kayla said, looking up and around the sky.

"It did, miss, right over us, are you okay?" the hand asked, while fidgeting with his ratty-looking black hat.

"I'm fine, Matt, thank you for asking." She pulled nervously at a strand of hair, the way this man was looking at her made her uncomfortable, it was like he was staring right through her.

"You can go back to work now, Matt, I will take Miss Price to her house."

"Yes, sir." Matt tipped his hat towards her and walked away to the barn.

"Why was he staring at me like that?" she asked as they neared the house.

"Maybe it's because you look like a contestant in a wet T-shirt contest."

Kayla followed his eyes down to her chest, her wet blouse clung to her large breasts like a second skin, her nipples were prominent as if they were trying to escape the confinement of her bra.

"Oh my God! I cannot believe that you let me stand here like this, why didn't you say something?"

"The truth is, I was enjoying the sight myself," he admitted…snickering.

"You are a pervert, Jake, did you know that?"

"If you say so, I'm not going to deny that I like what I see."

"It doesn't bother you one bit, does it?"

"Not a bit, now you had better get changed into some dry clothes."

"I will just as soon as you leave."

"You're not much fun at all."

"Out, pervert." She pointed to the door.

"I'm going." He turned to walk out but he had one more thing to say.

"By the way, did I mention that you would have won that wet T-shirt contest, had there been one?"

"Out!" she yelled, throwing a pillow at his head, narrowly missing.

Kayla shut and locked the door behind him. As she passed a mirror she noticed her blushing cheeks. She stripped off her wet clothes and ran a warm bubble bath, she soaked in the tub until her skin turned pink and wrinkled, the heat had drained her of all her energy. Instead of putting on her usual night shirt she just toweled off and climbed in under the crisp sheets. She quickly fell asleep.

Kayla's dream would be different this night, the man she had dreamt about for the past few months stepped slightly out of the shadows, she could see that he was wearing boots with spurs and he had a gun belt around his waist. Was he there to shoot her, she wondered.

Fear rushed through her body, making her shiver, but she was only frightened for a moment. He stood over her now, she could feel his breath on her neck. It was warm and sweet and at that very moment she knew that he would never hurt her.

"Kayla, Kayla, wake up."

Someone was shaking her by the shoulders and she could feel her dream man slipping away once again.

"Wait," she heard herself call out. She slowly opened her eyes.

"Kayla, are you all right?" It was Jake, he was sitting on the side of her bed, his shirt was un buttoned to his waist and a fine sheen of sweat covered his muscular chest.

"It's almost one in the afternoon, I've been knocking on the door trying to wake you for what seems like forever, when I looked through the window and saw you just lying there I thought... I thought...

"You thought what? I was dead?" A smile crossed her face.

"Maybe... You could have been."

You really do care about me." She sat up and threw her arms around Jake's neck, forgetting that she had not put on any clothing after her bath last night. Her naked breasts were now pressed up against Jake's hard body.

"I'm sorry, I forgot—"

Jake held his hand up to stop her from continuing. "That's okay," he told her, but it wasn't, it was not okay that she do that to him, how could she forget about not being dressed? How could she forget how much he wanted her?

"I shouldn't have come in, I was just worried about you." He pulled the sheet over her and stepped away from the bed.

"I know that you wouldn't take advantage of me, Jake."

He had to say something, he had to change the subject, he had to get his filthy mind off of her and her gorgeous body.

"I repaired the roof this morning. I would have thought the noise would have woke you, that must have been some dream that you were having."

"I don't recall dreaming." She said this in all honesty; for the moment she actually had forgotten about her dream man coming out of the shadows. Now Jake was the only man on her mind. She smiled at him.

Jake backed up against the door. "I have a lot of work to do, I had better get going."

"Wait." Kayla jumped up out of bed with the sheet wrapped around her. "Will you come over tonight?"

"I have a lot of work to do. That storm did some damage to the property. I could be real late."

"It doesn't matter how late, just stop by."

"All right, I'll see you later." Jake shut the door behind him. Curiosity was getting the best of him—why all of a sudden did she want him to come over?

Kayla dropped her sheet and quickly dressed, she couldn't understand why but she was suddenly in a great mood and tonight she was going to prove to Jake that she was capable of caring about someone and letting someone care for her as well, she planned to make him a wonderful dinner and then… Maybe six years of waiting for Jake would finally come to an end.

TWO

Jake knocked on the door at eight fifteen that evening. He was hot and sticky from the long day of working on the ranch and all he wanted to do was take a shower and go to bed, maybe sleep for a few days. But he had promised Kayla that he would stop by no matter what time it happened to be.

He leaned against the door frame while he waited for her to answer his knock.

When she finally opened the door she stood before him in a white negligee. She looked like an angel, absolutely beautiful.

"I thought you might not come."

"I told you it could be late." He put a hand over his mouth to hide a yawn.

Kayla shrugged and opened the door wide. "Come in and sit down," she ordered.

"I'm too filthy…" He tried to brush away some of the dirt that clung to his clothing.

"Don't argue with me." She pulled him through the door way. "Come in and sit down."

Jake found him a seat in the middle of the sofa, he knew that there was a chance he might fall asleep, he was so tired. Jake looked around the room noticing that the table was set for two and the only lighting in the room was candlelight.

"I hope you're hungry." She circled around behind the sofa, running her fingers along the back of it. Reaching Jake, she started to rub his neck. She could feel the tension in him.

He stopped her hand and held it for a moment. "What are you up to?" he asked suspiciously.

"I just wanted to do something special for you, to let you know how much I appreciate you and all the things you do for me and the ranch."

Jake was not sure what was happening here between the two of them, but now was just not a good time for it to be happening. He stood up with every intention of leaving. "I really need a shower, babe, can whatever this is about wait until morning?"

"No, it cannot wait. I have been planning this all day. I've cooked and you're going to sit down and eat, you can take your shower here."

"I don't have any clothes here."

"Yes, you do, I went down to your trailer and got some for you. They are already laid out in the bathroom, so go on and get cleaned up."

Kayla pulled him up from the sofa and patted him on the butt, shooing him off to get cleaned up like she would a child.

Jake closed the bathroom door and started the water. She was up to something. He was confused, he had been making passes at this woman for years and she blew him off every time; now all of a sudden she was the one making the passes.

Jake stood under the spray of the water and let the heat relax his tired muscles. He regretted having to get out but he could not stay in there forever; eventually the water would get cold or Kayla would come for him.

He turned off the water and pulled the curtain open, the steam was so heavy that he could not see. He reached blindly for his towel… He felt something and grabbed at it but it was Kayla he grabbed. She stood in front of him holding up a fluffy white towel.

"Looking for this?" she asked.

"What the hell are you doing in here?"

"Getting you a towel." She grinned.

"I can get my own towel. In case you haven't noticed, I am a grown man."

"Oh, I noticed," she said, looking over his naked body.

Jake grabbed the towel from her and wrapped it around his waist.

Kayla left the bathroom smiling, she had him rattled, that was for sure.

Jake dressed and sat down on the edge of the tub, he had to think for a moment. What was he going to do? He couldn't very well hide in there for the rest of the night. His attention focused on the window. He actually thought about sneaking out of the window; instead he took a deep breath and opened the door.

"It's about time, I thought you might have jumped out the window and run away."

Jake gave her a silly grin. "To be honest, the thought did cross my mind."

"So what changed it?"

"I'm hungry."

They sat together and ate the wonderful dinner that she had prepared, Jake scooted his chair away from the table and rubbed his hands over his belly.

"That was great, Kayla."

"Thank you."

"Would you find it rude of me to eat and run?"

"I would find it very rude of you to leave now, Jake. Why are you in such a hurry?"

"I'm tired, Kay, just very tired, I need some sleep."

"You could sleep here," she suggested.

"I guess I could sleep just as good on your sofa as I could in my own bed. Hell, I'm so tired I could sleep in the hog pen and not notice the stink."

She quickly dismissed his joke. "I don't think you understand what I'm saying, I want you to stay the night with me, in my room, in my bed, I want you to make love to me, Jake." She figured if anything would wake him up it would be that.

"What?"

"I want to make love, isn't that what you have been waiting for all these years?"

"I have wanted that for a long time," he admitted.

"Well, now is your chance."

"No," he said, not believing that answer had come from his lips. What was he thinking?

"What do you mean no?"

Kayla had been right about him wanting her, since the first time that he laid eyes on her six years ago, he rarely thought about anything else but being with her. As the years went by the lust had turned to love, he cared deeply for her and he would not take advantage of her. He knew that if he took her up on this, she would regret it in the morning.

"You told me yesterday that I was afraid to let someone love me, I'm trying to show you that I'm not afraid, love me now." She stepped into his arms.

"I do love you, Kay, I have loved you for a long time. If I take you to bed now and you reject me later it will kill me."

"Who's to say that will happen? Maybe we are meant to be and I have just been too stubborn to see that." She let her nightgown slip off of her shoulders and fall to the floor in a pool of silk around her ankles.

Jake scooped her up into his arms and carried her into the bedroom. He laid her down and sat on the side of the bed. She was beautiful. He bent down and took her mouth in a passionate kiss, then he took her breasts in his hands and kneaded them lovingly. Kayla sighed deeply and pulled him closer to her.

"I love you, Kayla," he whispered in her ear. He felt her tense up when he said it. "Do you love me?" he asked.

"I care deeply for you, Jake, and I want to make love to you."

"But you don't love me?"

"What has love got to do with this? Don't you want me anymore, Jake? Have I waited too long?"

Jake took Kayla's hand and moved it over to the front of his jeans so that she could feel his straining erection.

"This is how much I want you, Kayla, but even so, I just can't make love to you tonight, it wouldn't be fair to either one of us."

"What are you babbling about?"

"It wouldn't be right, we would be using each other and we would both regret it in the morning and our friendship would be changed forever. I don't want that to happen."

He took her face in his hands and wiped a single tear from her eye, he then planted a kiss firmly on her forehead.

"If you ever decide that you love me like I love you, call me and I will come running." Jake covered her with the sheet and slowly walked out, closing the door softly behind him.

Standing on the front porch he took a deep breath of fresh air, he suddenly wanted to kick himself. He dreamed of hearing Kayla ask him to make love to her and now it finally had happened and he turned her down, how stupid could he be? He kicked at the dirt.

He knew Kayla too well, she would have liked it at the time but she would have regretted it in the morning.

The next morning Kayla woke up ready to get started on her new flowerbed.

After Jake had left she cried a few tears, mostly just feeling sorry for herself but still finding herself somewhat relieved that Jake had turned her down. Maybe he knew her better than she knew herself. It would have been unfair to him, she knew that he loved her and she loved him, just not the same way, and Jake was a good man. He deserved a woman to love him the same way he loved her, and she was just not that woman.

Kayla dressed and decided to work off her extra energy by collecting the rocks for her flowerbed border from the top of the hill. She decided to walk up the hill, pile her rocks and then return later with her four wheeler and trailer to haul them down with.

By the time Kayla reached the top of the hill she was short of breath and slightly dizzy. The view from the top of the hill was spectacular. She wished that the house had been built up there so that she could sit on the porch and have that same view all day long.

She began searching for rocks, she had picked a few and set them in a pile when she spotted one that was a bit larger than the others. She thought it would make a perfect centerpiece, the rock was tall and thick, it had moss cascading down the side of it, reminding Kayla of a waterfall. She walked closer to the rock; she could see that it had something carved into its surface: the letters *KIN*. She reached out and touched it, she felt a jolt, almost as if she had been shocked. She quickly pulled her hand back and let it fall limply to her side. She sat silent for a moment until she heard someone calling her name.

Kayla walked to the edge of the hill and looked over the side. There she saw her chubby friend Shelly looking up at her. She had stopped halfway up the hill and was holding on to her side, breathing heavily.

"What are you doing up there?" Shelly yelled.

"Gathering rocks, come on up."

"No thanks, why don't you come on down?"

It was clear to Kayla that her friend was not at all happy about being on that hill.

"It's not going to kill you to get a little bit of exercise."

"It might," Shelly replied.

"I'll be right down." Kayla took a quick look back at the rock. The letters jumped out at her again. She turned and all but ran down the hill until she stood in front of her friend.

"What did you say you were doing up there?"

"Gathering rocks for the new flowerbed."

"Oh! You and your flowerbeds! Don't you have enough? And as for rocks, there are plenty of those down here, take a look around." Shelly just could not understand her friend's fascination with rocks and flowers.

Kayla picked up a small pebble and held it to Shelly's face. "These are pebbles, I need rocks." She tossed the pebble at Shelly's feet.

"Ouch." Not that it hurt, but she wanted Kayla to think it did.

"Sorry," she said, even though she wasn't. "What brings you here anyway?"

"Do I need a reason to see my best friend?"

"No. But there must be a reason."

"I just thought that you might want to get some pizza."

"After the time I just had getting up that hill the last thing I need is pizza."

"Okay, see you later." Shelly turned to walk away.

"Wait, I didn't say no, I just said that I didn't need it." Kayla grabbed her friend's hand, pulling her along to the bottom of the hill.

"Kayla, if you're lucky I won't fall and roll into your house."

Kayla didn't like it when Shelly made fun of her weight, she wasn't that heavy.

When they reached the bottom of the hill Jake was there to meet them. "Hello, ladies."

"Well, helloooooooo, Jake." Shelly stepped up to Jake to flirt as she usually did. She was happily married but she couldn't seem to resist flirting with the man.

Jake gave Shelly a good long look and a silly grin before he turned to Kayla. "How are you this morning?"

"I'm good...and you were right about last night," she added.

"That's what I thought."

"Excuse me," Shelly butted in. "What's this about last night?"

"Oh, Shelly, I almost forgot you were here," Kayla said.

"Well, that's a fine how do you do." She was truly offended by that. "Never mind, you can make it up to me by telling me what happened last night."

Jake could see that he needed to get Kayla off of the hot seat if only for a moment. "Here are the receipts from yesterday." Jake held out the papers for her to take, being careful not to touch her silky skin as she took them from him.

"Would you please wait for me in the house, Shelly?" Kayla asked.

"I just wanted to know about last night, is that so terrible?"

Jake touched Shelly's hand. "You just go on in the house now and don't worry about what did or didn't happen last night."

"Jake, if I weren't a married woman I'd be after you," she admitted.

"If you weren't a married woman I'd let you catch me."

"Yuck." Kayla thought that she was going to be sick, maybe she was a little jealous.

Shelly finally relented and went into the house. She knew that she would eventually get the truth out of Kayla.

"This is something, I all but begged you to sleep with me last night and you turned me down, but yet Shelly winks at you and you're almost ready to jump into bed with her."

Jake found it humorous that Kayla was jealous of a little flirting between friends. "I only say those things because it makes her feel good, it's good for her self-esteem."

"Yeah, well, she has a husband to make her feel good."

"Sometimes a woman needs to hear nice things from a man other than her husband."

"Why are you so up to date on what a woman needs?"

"I'm not looking for a fight, Kayla," Jake backed away.

"I'm not trying to fight with you," she lied.

"It sure sounds like it." Jake looked at the ground and kicked a clod of dirt with the toe of his boot. "Just for the record, I kicked myself all the way home last night, I even thought about coming back." The truth was he fought himself to keep from going back and making passionate love to her; instead he went home and took the coldest shower that he had ever taken before in his life.

"I'm still not completely sure why you turned me down."

Jake took her hands in his. "Because, my dear, I am in love with you and if and when you feel the same way, then that will be the right time for us to make love."

And just like that he walked away, leaving her at the front door of the house.

As soon as she walked in Shelly bombarded her with questions, her eyes were big and bright and she was acting like a teenage girl about to hear some juicy gossip. "So what happened, or didn't happen, last night between you and Jake?"

"Nothing happened." Kayla walked past her and dropped the receipts down on the desktop, then she sat down on the sofa. She really didn't want to get into this but she knew that Shelly was not going to let it go so easily.

"That was not about nothing out there, sister. Now tell me what went down with Jake," she demanded.

"Okay, you really want to know so badly, I tried to seduce him last night," she admitted.

"What do you mean you tried?"

"Just what I said, I tried and he shot me down."

"Why would he turn you down? He loves you."

"How do you know he loves me?"

"A person would have to be blind not to see that Jake is in love with you."

"Call me blind then because I didn't know it until last night."

Shelly paced the floor. "I can't believe he told you no."

"Well, believe it."

"It's because you don't love him back, that's the only reason he said no."

"It wouldn't have been fair to either of us because no, I don't love him back."

"Couldn't you try? He is such a wonderful man."

"I know he is, but I just don't love him like that." Kayla laid her head back on the sofa and closed her eyes.

"Did you see him naked?" Shelly asked excitedly.

"I can't believe you just asked me that." Kayla tried to hide her smile.

"You did."

"I wouldn't tell you if I had."

"Oh yes, you will." Shelly pushed Kayla to the floor and began to tickle her without mercy.

Kayla screamed in protest. "Okay, I give up, I saw him naked," she confessed. She felt like she was going to pee her pants.

"I knew it." Shelly sat back in her chair while Kayla tried to compose herself. "What does he look like?"

"I'll tell you one thing, he is big all over." She giggled.

"I knew it, I knew it."

"Can we change the subject?"

"Sure, I don't know if I told you this but I am spending the night tonight."

"You are?" Strange, Kayla could not seem to remember inviting her to stay the night, but since when did that ever stop Shelly? She usually did what she wanted. And of course she was always welcome.

"Billy has to work tonight and I don't want to stay home alone. I don't know how you can stand to be in this big house by yourself every night, out here with no neighbors except for Jake that is, don't you ever get scared?

"Not usually, but now that you have brought it up, did I tell you about the footprints outside of my window?"

"No. Do you have a peeping Tom, or a peeping Jake?"

"I'm sure it wasn't Jake." She wouldn't be worried if she thought it had been Jake walking around by her bedroom window, she may not be in love with him but she trusted him with her life, just like her father had.

"I wouldn't worry about it too much, Jake is just down the drive, he will take care of you."

"I know he will, but just the thought of someone being right out side my bedroom window gives me the creeps." Kayla got a chill up her spine.

Two hours later the two women sat in front of the television set eating warm pizza and watching the movie they had rented.

"So, did I tell you about the great rock I found up on the hill?"

Kayla knew Shelly didn't want to hear about the rock but she just couldn't stop thinking about it all day and she needed to talk to someone about it.

"What could be so great about a rock?" *Darn*, she thought, *here we go again with her stupid rock stories, can't she think about something else to talk about?*

"It's perfect for my centerpiece, but I am not sure if I want to move it or not."

"Why not?"

"It has the letters *KIN* carved into it and when I touched it I got a strange feeling, kind of like a shock... What if someone is buried under that rock?"

"I don't think anyone is buried under it, I'm sure some kid just carved his name in it, some kid that can't spell." She chuckled "Apparently you don't know that in the old days Ken was spelled Kin."

"No, I didn't know that, Sherlock, since when did you become such an expert on the old days?"Shelly looked at her friend in bewilderment. What was going on with her, she wondered.

"Kayla, you have a very vivid imagination. Even if that rock is a gravestone, that guy underneath it is very dead, and what can a dead man do to you?"

Shelly had a point.

"You're right, what can a dead man do to me?"

THREE

Kayla woke up screaming at the top of her lungs. The bedside clock read two fifteen in the morning. She was drenched in sweat and breathing heavily as if she had just run a marathon.

Shelly was at her side within seconds. "What's the matter, Kayla?" She shook her by her shoulders.

"I...I had a really bad dream."

"What was your dream about, honey?"

"The same dream that I have been having every night for the past few months." Kayla sat up in bed and turned on the lamp. She proceeded to tell Shelly about the nightly dreams. "I'm sitting up in bed, only it isn't my bed. This man is standing in the corner of the room. So far he had been staying in the shadows. At first I was scared, but I know that he will not hurt me, but—"

"Calm down, you don't have to talk so fast."

Kayla took a deep breath. "I honestly believe that this dream means something, tonight the man was about to come out of the shadows and speak to me for the first time when—"

"I dream about Mel Gibson all the time; does that mean I will meet him?" Shelly interrupted.

"I'm serious!" Kayla yelled, shocking her best friend.

"I'm sorry, I'm listening."

"Okay, so the man comes out of the shadows, he is wearing

an old pair of jeans and a plaid western shirt, and his boots have spurs on them."

"Does this dream get kinky?"

Ignoring Shelly's question, Kayla continued with her story. "He steps out of the shadows, I can't see his face real good but I get this weird feeling, I think he wants to make love to me—"

"It does get kinky. Yeah!"

"Will you stop interrupting me, he doesn't make love to me," She swallowed hard, "because when he does get close to me he whispers that someone has shot him and that I could be next, then he falls face first onto the bed, bleeding, and he dies practically in my arms." Tears streamed down her face and Shelly could tell that this dream was really upsetting to her friend.

"I think you're getting upset over nothing, it was just a silly dream."

"I don't think it's silly at all, I think that someone might be trying to kill me."

"No, who would want to kill you? Don't try to make it real, just a dream, repeat after me… just a dream."

"What about the footprints in the flowerbed, right under this very window?" Kayla pointed to her bedroom window. Shelly got goose bumps.

"I'm sure it was just one of the ranch hands trying to get a good look at the sexy boss lady."

"Maybe. I have been thinking about getting a watchdog, a big one like a Doberman."

"That's a good idea…even though I am sure that there is nothing to worry about. I will help you look for a dog in the morning if you want to, but now can we please go back to sleep?"

"I'd rather stay up."

"But it's still dark out side," Shelly whined.

"I'm sure that I can't go back to sleep, not now." Kayla stood up out of bed. "I'd like to take a shower, I'm sticky with sweat."

"I'll make us some coffee while you shower."

"Thank you, you're a good friend." Kayla pinched her friend's cheeks, just like her Aunt Vera used to do to her when she was a little girl.

"You would do the same for me." Shelly returned the cheek pinch.

"In a heartbeat," Kayla admitted.

As Shelly stood at the kitchen sink filling the carafe with water she gazed out the window into the dark night, she fixed her gaze at the top of the hill just as lightning struck and lit up the sky, giving her a clear view of the top of the hill. She gasped and the glass carafe slipped from her hand to the floor, shattering into a dozen pieces.

Kayla had heard the crash and came running into the kitchen. "What happened?"

Shelly jumped, she turned around and looked directly into her friend's eyes, hoping that she couldn't see her fear. "The lightning scared me, I'm sorry about the coffee pot," she stammered.

"It's okay, don't worry about it, I have another one just like it." Kayla grabbed the broom from the closet and started to sweep up the shards of glass.

While Kayla did that Shelly ran from room to room, making sure that the doors and windows were all locked.

"What are you doing?"

"Just checking the locks, can't be too careful, you know."

"What happened to you? And don't tell me the lightning scared you, it was more than that."

"It was just the ligh—"

"Stop right there," Kayla cut her off. "Tell me what happened."

Shelly knew that Kayla would not give up on her, she had to tell her the truth.

"Okay, I was looking out the window when the lightning struck and it lit up the top of the hill and…and…"

"What? Spit it out, Shelly."

"I saw a man standing on the hill."

"What man?"

"I don't know what man, I couldn't see that clearly, but I know that I saw a man on the hill, it looked like he was watching me."

Kayla's eyes went glassy and a bead of sweat appeared on her top lip. "He's here to kill me. The man in my dreams was right, the man you saw is here to kill me."

"Stop talking like that, no one wants to kill you, maybe I didn't even see a man, I could have imagined it."

"What you saw was real, Shelly, or else you wouldn't have been running around here locking the doors and windows."

"Look, I don't know if it was real or not, but I do know that I am calling Jake right now."

"It won't matter, Jake can't stop him."

Shelly already had the number dialed and it was ringing.

Kayla flopped down on the sofa, half expecting a man to burst through the door wielding a gun and shooting her dead where she sat.

A man did burst in but it was Jake. "I ran as fast as I could. What's going on?"

"You're just wasting your time, Jake," Kayla said. She walked into the next room.

"What is her problem?"

"She thinks that someone is out to kill her," Shelly told him as she looked him over head to toe.

"That's ridiculous, who would want to kill her?" Jake couldn't help but notice the way Shelly was watching him, then he realized that he had run out of his house wearing only boxer shorts and his boots—what a sight he must have been.

Shelly proceeded to tell Jake about Kayla's dreams and the man she thought she saw on top of the hill.

Jake found Kayla staring out of the window of her father's

study. He walked up behind her and put his arms around her shoulders. They both stared out into the dark night.

"The man that Shelly saw wants me dead," she told him.

"Shelly told me about your nightmares, but that's all they are, sweetheart, just bad dreams." He stroked her hair.

"I knew that you wouldn't understand, the man in my dreams was warning me about the man that Shelly saw on the hill, the same man that was in my flowerbeds, the man that wants to kill me."

Jake didn't know what to say to her. How could he make her feel safe when the fact was that he didn't know if she was safe, what if Shelly really did see a man on the hill? What if someone was after Kayla?

"Shelly and I have discussed it and one of us will be with you at all times, just until we figure this out."

Kayla turned to face him. "I can't ask you to do that, you both have your own lives."

"You're not asking, we are telling you, and that is that."

While Jake and Shelly tried to organize a schedule so that Kayla would not be alone for the next few days, she drifted off into a light sleep. Jake watched as she slept. Her lips were curled up into a slight smile, she looked so peaceful. He only looked away for a moment but when he looked back at her, her expression was troubled, he waited to see if she would wake on her own, when she opened her eyes she looked at Jake and began to cry. Jake jumped up and ran over to her. He held her tenderly in his arms.

"You had another dream. Do you want to tell me about it?"

Kayla thought for a moment and decided to tell him about it. "The stranger… He walked towards me, I heard a loud bang, at first it sounded like a firecracker but it was a gunshot. He fell into my lap, there was blood all over me, his blood. He told me to run as fast as I could, so I did. I ran and ran and that's when I woke up… I should have stayed, maybe I could have saved him."

Jake could see that this dream had really upset her, she was acting as if it were real, and it was starting to scare him.

Kayla believed that her dream was a message and she had to do whatever she could to sort it out. She looked around the room. The sun had come up and Shelly was gone.

"Where did Shelly go?"

"I sent her home for a while, she needed to see her husband. She'll be back around noon. Until then I'm all yours."

"Don't you need to go to work, or at least put some clothes on?" She looked down at his red silk boxer shorts. "I never figured you for a silk kind of guy."

Jake turned red from embarrassment. "I was in a hurry, I just put my boots on and ran when Shelly called."

"Well, it's a good thing you don't sleep in the nude." She chuckled.

"Of course it's not like I haven't seen you naked before." She thought back to the night before when Jake climbed out of the shower. She got slightly flustered thinking about it.

"Yeah! That was funny...not." Truth be told, he was still a little shaken up over that incident. "And by the way, I don't need to do anything until Shelly gets here."

"Don't be silly, Jake, you should go on with your day. Besides, you said yourself it was only a dream, I'm not scared anymore so you don't have to babysit me," she insisted.

"I think maybe we should just stay in the house so you can get some rest."

"Come on, Jake, I would like to go up the hill and gather some more rocks for the new flowerbed." Kayla batted her long lashes at him.

"Lady, you do make it hard to say no to you. I do, however, need to put some clothes on before we head outside." Jake went up to Kayla's father's closet and borrowed some jeans and an old plaid shirt; they were a little big on him but they would do for today.

He hoped that Kayla wouldn't be too upset seeing him in her father's clothes. When he came down the stairs Kayla gave him a strange look but she said nothing because the phone rang, taking her mind off of it.

"Hello!" Shelly was on the other end of line telling her that she was going to be a little late but she would be there as soon as possible.

"Don't worry about it, I'll see you soon."

"What did she say?" Jake was stomping his foot like a child.

Kayla ignored him and slipped a house key in her pant pocket and walked out the front door. Jake followed.

"What did she say?" he asked again.

"She said that she would be a little late."

"And you weren't going to tell me about that."

"I didn't think it was necessary. I overreacted last night, I was really scared and now I realize it was silly to be so scared. No one is out to get me and I will be fine, go to work, the ranch needs your attention more than I do."

"I'm glad you're feeling better, but it would make me feel better if I stayed with you, at least until Shelly arrives."

"Whatever you want to do, Jake." She couldn't help but stare at him, he was wearing her dead father's clothes. She loved that old plaid shirt on her father, for months she had been going to his room, planning to give his clothes to goodwill but each time she just couldn't bear to do it, the thought of getting rid of his things was just too hard for her.

"Does it bother you that I'm wearing his clothes?"

"It's not about the clothes, Jake, I just miss him so much." She couldn't help it, tears started to flow. Jake didn't know what to say, nothing could bring him back, he pulled out his bandanna and handed it to her. She dabbed at her tears.

"You know it won't hurt his feelings if you get rid of his things, he would understand."

"I just feel like I would be betraying him."

Jake stepped up to be directly in front of her. "Your father's

38

memory lives in here and here." He put a hand to her head and then to her heart. "He will always be with you."

Kayla stood straighter and tried to regain her composure. "I know he is in a better place and with Mom. I guess I'm just feeling sorry for myself."

"There is nothing wrong with missing your parents, you have that right."

They continued walking up the hill.

"Shelly will be here soon, you really don't have to stay with me."

"I'll stay."

"Really, Jake, I will be fine." They trudged upward until they reached the top of the hill.

Jake took a seat on an old fallen tree to catch his breath. "When did I get so old?" he asked himself.

"Fine, since you're determined to stay here you might as well be doing something useful."

"Yes, ma'am, what would you like me to do first?"

"You could start by —"

Kayla was interrupted by one of the ranch hands running towards them yelling to Jake, "Boss, the cattle have broke through the west side fence again, we need your help."

"Can't you guys handle it? That's why I hired you." He was obviously upset by the intrusion.

"Normally we could handle it but Matt and Skinny are both sick in bed today, we really need you, boss."

Jake looked at Kayla, then back to the ranch hand she knew only as old Buck.

"Go ahead, Jake, I'll be fine, really," she reassured.

"I don't think it's a good idea to leave you alone."

"You don't have a choice, this ranch is our livelihood, you do what needs to be done."

She had a point, the bills had to get paid, and she was the boss.

"I'll be fine, Shelly will be here shortly, and when you're done we will have supper together, how does that sound?"

"It sounds good, but why don't you come with me," he urged, knowing that herding cattle and mending fences was not big on her to do list.

"It's been a long time since I've been on a horse, you go on, I'll be fine."

He knew he needed to go but he had an impending feeling of doom, like if he left her he might never see her again.

He kissed her lightly on the cheek before turning away. She watched as he ran down the hill to the barn, jumped on his horse and headed west.

Old Buck tore off behind him in an old, beat-up truck loaded with fencing materials.

A feeling of dread washed over her. She chose to ignore it and knelt in the dirt in front of the moss-covered rock that had held her attention the day before. It seemed to have some hypnotic hold over her.

"Do you find that rock interesting?"

Kayla whirled around at the sound of the voice, it was a voice that she had heard before.

"Matt, I thought that you were sick in bed." Hadn't that been what old Buck had just said?

"Oh, I'm sick, sick and tired of getting the raw end of the deal, I'm sick of people stealing what belongs to me and my family," he snarled at her.

Kayla was puzzled, she could smell liquor on his breath, which could explain why he was making no sense.

"Has someone stole something from you?" she asked.

"I'm talking about this ranch, it belongs to me," he told her.

Kayla hadn't been impressed with this kid the first time she met him and now she was really starting to get irritated by him.

Kayla turned her attention back to the rock. "This ranch belongs to me," she stated.

"Not for long, it will be mine in just a few short days," he taunted.

That was it, she was plum mad now, who did he think he was? Jake was going to have to fire him immediately. If he was lucky he wouldn't get socked in the jaw as well.

"What are you talking about?" she asked. She looked Matt up and down. She noticed his boots, they looked to be about the size of the footprints she'd found in her flowerbed.

Her anger was beginning to turn into fear. Was he the man who had been watching through her window? The man whom Shelly had seen on top of the hill? Was he the man who was going to kill her?

"This ranch belonged to my family once," he told her.

She tried not to let him see her fear. "As far as I know this ranch has always been in my family."

"Your family stole it from mine, and I'm here to get it back." Matt had noticed the interest Kayla seemed to have in the rock, she looked from him to the rock as if the rock had some magic power that might save her from him.

"Do you know who is buried under that rock?" he asked.

"Who?" Kayla didn't want to act too interested but she couldn't help herself. From the minute she saw it she thought someone might actually be buried there, and now this crazy man was telling her it was true, she had to know.

"A man named Kin Parsons, he's the rotten son of a gun that stole the ranch from my family, he was a cattle thief. To make a long story short, this is my ranch and I will have it back."

How did this man seem to know so much about the past? Was he just making it all up? Or was what he saying true? It couldn't all be true. That ranch was hers and had been in her family for over one hundred years.

"Matt, I don't know and I don't really care what this man Parsons did to your family but this land is mine and has been for over a hundred years. It's legally mine and it will stay that way, like it or not."

"I'll own it before the week is over," he told her, spitting a wad of chewing tobacco at her feet.

"Over my dead body." *Stupid, drunk idiot,* she thought. Where was Shelly? She should have been there by now.

"Who is the ranch willed to?" he asked.

"None of your business."

"Let me guess, if you die Jake gets the ranch."

Kayla stood stock-still, it felt as if her heart was going to jump out of her chest. How could he know that?

"I bet you're wondering how I know this. I know because Jake is going to sell it to me dirt cheap when you're dead and gone."

"Why would you buy a ranch you just told me you owned?"

"Like you said, lady, legally it's yours, and it might look a little suspicious if Jake just handed over the deed."

"If I were to die Jake would not sell this ranch, he loves it."

"Jake has his own ranch, just on the west side of this one."

"I don't believe you, he would have told me if he had his own place."

"Ever wonder why he's always so tired? He's running two ranches, where do you think your cattle are going? Over to Jake's place. You're paying for his cattle. Ever wonder why he needs so much lumber? Hell, lady, he's built a house that you paid for. How can you be so blind? Jake has been stealing from you and your daddy for the past six years."

"Jake wouldn't steal from me. I don't believe a word you're saying, Daddy would have known if Jake were a thief."

"He did find out… Jake took care of him."

"Are you saying that Jake killed my daddy? Because he died from a heart attack."

"It doesn't take much to make a sick old man have a heart attack." Matt laughed wildly, spitting another wad of gross black tobacco at her feet again.

"You're a lying bastard." Kayla lunged at Matt, he grabbed her and pushed her to the ground. She hit her head on the moss-covered rock. When she saw the blood from her wound, she fainted.

Matt stood over her, he felt for a pulse, she was just knocked out, but Matt was going to make sure that she didn't wake up. He picked up a rock and raised it over his head. Just as he was about to smash Kayla's skull, a sudden gust of wind came up, dust swirled around his feet and up his body into his eyes, forcing him to close them. When it was all over and he was able to open his eyes he saw that Kayla was gone. He looked all around. She was out cold, where could she have gone? She didn't have time to escape. Matt noticed that the mossy rock was gone as well. The rock that Kin Parsons was buried under was gone and there was nothing left but a big, gaping hole, a hole wide enough and deep enough to be a grave.

Matt dropped his would-e murder weapon and ran back to the barn. He pulled out a bottle of whiskey that he had hidden under a hay bale and downed it in three long swallows. As far as he was concerned if there was any time he needed a drink, it was at that very moment. There was something weird happening. Kayla couldn't have just vanished into thin air, it just wasn't possible.

FOUR

1876

Kayla struggled to open her eyes. After the dizziness stopped and she was able to see clearly she found herself lying on her back staring at the ceiling. She soon realized that it was not her ceiling she was staring at. This one appeared to be made of logs.

She sat up in the bed and looked around. Nothing she saw looked familiar to her; it all looked like a scene out of a history book, or one of those rooms in a museum, like the ones her parents used to take her to when she was young.

Kayla held her aching head. She couldn't ever remember having a headache this bad in her life.

Across the room sat a dresser that looked as if it were brand new, but it couldn't have been because they didn't make furniture like that anymore, and they hadn't for a long time. She thought that whoever it belonged to must have been an antique collector.

Kayla sat up but quickly lay back down when the room started to spin. She could not remember what had happened that would have given her such a horrible headache.

She leaned her head back against the headboard and it was then that she realized she was not alone in the room.

There was a shadow, someone standing in the corner of the room, by the doorway. The shadow moved closer to her and she could see that it was a man. He was wearing faded jeans and an old western shirt, he wore cowboy boots with spurs.

She wondered, who wore spurs anymore?

The jingle of the metal spurs grew louder as he got closer to her. An inner voice told her that she should be scared of this man but oddly enough she was not. Even though she had yet to see his face she sensed that he was harmless.

"I must be dreaming again," she whispered.

"What did you say?" his voice boomed, making her head throb even more. She wondered if that was what a hangover felt like, because if it was she was glad that she was not a drinker.

"Who are you? And where am I?"

"My name is Kin and you are in my home."

"Well, that explains why nothing looks familiar, but it doesn't explain how I got here."

"I found you at my front door this morning, your head was bleeding so I brought you in and bandaged it up."

Kayla felt for the bandage. "Okay, now I know why I have such a pounding headache, but how did I get hurt and how did I end up at your door?"

"I can't tell you that, I just know that I couldn't leave you out there to bleed to death."

You could have taken me to a hospital, she thought. "Thank you!" She settled back in the bed and shut her eyes briefly.

"What is your name?" he asked, this time his voice being much softer.

"Kayla. What did you say your name was?"

"Kin. Where are you from, Kayla?"

She heard what he had said but it still hadn't registered in her mind that his name was the same as the name carved on her rock. "I'm from here," was all she said.

"I'm sure I would have seen you before now. And I've never seen a lady wear clothing like that before around these parts."

SHARON HENDRYX MCDANIEL

Kayla looked down at herself. "You have never seen a woman wear jeans and a tank top before?" *My God! Have I ended up that far from home?* "Where exactly are we?" she asked.

"We are at my ranch, about seven miles from the town of McAlester, Oklahoma. And no, I have never seen a woman wear britches, and underwear on the outside for all to see."

"It's not underwear, it's called a tank top." She grew defensive.

"I realize that I don't get out much but the only women that I ever see dressed like that are the ones that get paid for it, know what I mean?"

"I'm not sure that I do."

"To put it plain and simple, only the whores that work out of the saloon wear clothing like that."

Oh no, he didn't just call her a whore... Did he?

"I beg your pardon, I am not a whore, and for your information a lot of women dress like this." She was good and angry now, she wished this jerk would just take a step closer and come out of the shadows so she could see his face clearly, she wanted to see whom she was about to tell off.

"Do you have any idea how you might have gotten that bump on your head, Kayla..."

"Price, my name is Kayla Price, and no I do not know how it happened and how I got here, but I too live about seven miles from town so I must be close to home."

"If you're telling the truth then we must be neighbors."

"I have no reason to lie, and if I'd known I would end up here I would have been more careful, that's for damn sure."

"Strong language for a lady."

He walked over to the antique dresser, where he rinsed out a washcloth in an old water basin that sat atop it. He stepped closer to her, his face finally out of the shadows. The sight of him almost took her breath away. He sat on the side of the bed and washed her head wound and then applied a fresh bandage. Suddenly she realized why he was so familiar to her.

46

"It's you." She grabbed at his wrist.

"Yes, it's me." He looked at her as if she were loony. "Have we met before?"

"Yes... No, you'll think I'm crazy if I tell you."

"I already do, so you might as well tell me."

She let go of his wrist. "All right, I've been dreaming about you for months now, you wear the same clothes as you are now and I believe we were in this very room." She glanced around nervously.

"You must have gotten brain damage from that bump to your head. You could have only been dreaming of me if we had met before, and I'm sure that I would remember meeting you , especially if you had ever been in my bed."

"I never said I was in your bed, I said that we were in this room. And I have been dreaming of you but we have never met before."

"I'm flattered." He fluttered his eyelashes at her and stood up, tossing the bloody washcloth into the water basin.

"Don't be flattered."

"Don't feel bad, sweetheart, lot's of women dream of bedding me."

"I beg your pardon... I don't dream of bedding you," she lied.

"You don't have to beg... Was I good?"

"Good at what?"

"Making love, did I please you?"

Kayla couldn't believe what she was hearing. "I did not dream of bedding you, I dreamed that you were murdered and you died in my arms and nothing more."

"Nothing more, that's a pretty heavy dream to have about someone you don't know, or someone you do know for that matter." He fiddled with the bloody rag again. "I like the other dream better, you know, the one where we made love."

"I never had that dream." Oh, this man was beginning to frustrate her. "Like I said, you were shot in the back and you fell into my arms and told me that I should run, you warned me that I would be the next to die."

Kin asked himself why he felt the need to comfort this woman but he had no good answer. She just looked so miserable that he had to do something.

He drew closer to her. "It was just a dream…more of a nightmare, but not real."

"That's what my friends keep telling me."

"You should listen to your friends… So you say that you're from around here?"

"You're changing the subject."

"Damn right I'm changing the subject. Do you have any family, Kayla?"

"None living." She twisted a lock of hair around her index finger.

"So you're not related to Doc Price? Do you know Doc Price?"

"I can't say that I do." Kayla reached down and pulled an old, ratty quilt up over her, it seemed to be getting a little chilly in the old cabin.

"If you don't know Doc then you can't be from close by, everyone knows Doc."

"Well, I don't," she snipped at him.

He sat on the edge of the bed and looked straight into her eyes. "Have you remembered anything about that bump on your head?"

"No." Her eyes met his. She thought how handsome he was. She wondered if she was blushing because she could feel the heat in her face.

"Nothing at all?"

"I can't remember anything about how I got here with a knot on my head."

Kayla lay back in the bed and closed her eyes. She thought hard about what might have happened. Slowly some things started coming back to her.

"I fell down… I think I might have been arguing with someone and the next thing I know is I woke up here…in your bed."

"Someone had to have brought you here, it must have been the closest place, you did say you live nearby."

"I remember being on the top of the hill behind my house, my house would have been the closest place to take me. Why didn't they take me to my house?"

"Hell, lady, I don't know." He was ready to get rid of this nuisance, she was nice to look at but a bit of a loon.

"Where did you get all of these antiques?" She surveyed the room.

Again with the questions. He liked her better when she was lying there unconscious and quiet.

"What are you talking about?"

"You know, the old dresser and this bedframe, they don't make them like this anymore."

"You don't like them?" he asked, acting offended, but really he didn't give a rat's ass what she thought of his furnishings.

"I like them very much, they just don't make them like this anymore."

"I just bought this stuff last week, the salesman said it was the newest furniture on the market." *Damn,* he thought, *got snookered again.*

Kayla rustled around a bit, trying to get comfortable.

"Are you sure your alright?" he asked.

"I'll be okay, I wish this headache would go away." She sat up, suddenly aware that she needed to take care of some business. "Where is your bathroom?"

He looked at her with a look of confusion.

"I bathe outside," he told her.

"I don't think you understand, I have to pee." She was desperate now, she felt like she was about to pop.

Silly woman, he thought.

49

"Out the door and to the left about two hundred feet."

Kayla looked at him with wide eyes, was he saying what she thought he was saying?

"Are you telling me that you have an outhouse?"

"Unless you prefer to squat behind a bush, but I wouldn't advise that, snake might sink his teeth into your bare ass." He shook off the thought of seeing her bare behind. *Pull yourself together, man.*

"Very funny, snake, outhouse, no running water, you have to have running water."

"Sure, I've got running water."

"Thank God, I actually thought that you were serious about the outhouse."

"I am."

"But…you just said you had running water."

"I do, there is a little creek about fifty yards from the backdoor."

"Oh you…you… I don't have time to mess with you right now, I need to find that outhouse…fast." Kayla pushed him out of her way, trying her best not to lose control over her bladder, that would be embarrassing.

After Kayla relieved herself and stepped out of the outhouse she took her time walking back to the little cabin. She saw Kin leaning against the frame of the front door. He had a stick of straw between his lips—apparently he didn't know what a toothpick was either.

Oddly enough Kayla found it sexy and she couldn't seem to look away from him.

"See something you like?" he asked her.

"It's very pretty out here. How much land do you have?"

"About nine hundred acres or so."

"Really? I have nine hundred acres."

"Surely you don't take care of that land yourself."

"Not that it's any of your business but I have several men that work the land. Jake is in charge, he's wonderful." What was she trying to do, make him jealous?

"So you and this Jake are…" He was fishing for answers, but why? Why did he care what Jake was to her? He didn't know her, he didn't like her, instead of asking questions he should have been trying to get rid of her as fast as he could.

"Jake and I are just friends."

What man in his right mind would be just friends with a beautiful woman like her?

"I'd like to see your ranch, where is it?"

"I already told you, seven miles west of town."

"Yes, but what town?"

"McAlester." She could have sworn that she had already told him this.

"It isn't possible because I live seven miles west of town. You must be confused."

"I believe I know where I live."

"Well, lady, I have met the neighbors to both sides of me and you are not one of them."

"I know you would like to think I'm confused but I am not. I know where I live."

"I don't doubt that you live somewhere nearby, obviously you have seen me before."

"Only in my dreams have I ever seen you before," she insisted. "And I'm starting to wish I hadn't seen you then." She turned her back on him to survey the land she stood on; it was very familiar.

"You are a feisty one," he told her while checking out her backside.

"I am not feisty, I'm just right."

"You strike me as one of those women who think they have to be right all of the time. We don't have many women like that around these parts, them are usually found in the big cities."

"Oh, them are, are they?" she mocked his bad grammar.

"I know what happened." Kin snapped his fingers. "You planned this whole thing just to get my attention."

"That's absurd, like I would knock myself in the head just to meet you, and if I had done that, I wouldn't still be here after meeting you, I would have left long ago. You are the most arrogant man I have ever met, and I don't even know your last name."

"Excuse me for not properly introducing myself, Kin Parsons is the name." He held out his hand to her but she didn't accept it. Her mouth gaped open as she stared at him.

"You couldn't be Kin Parsons."

"That's what my dear sweet ma named me, so it must be true."

"He is dead, I saw his headstone."

"I'm very much alive." He pulled her hands to his chest so that she could feel him. He was very real, and very solid. She pulled her hands away from him.

"No, I saw your headstone, you are dead," she insisted.

"Could a dead man walk? Could a dead man talk? Could a dead man do this?" He pulled her into his arms and planted a firm kiss on her pouting lips. Her lips parted, their tongues dueled with each other. Kayla had never been kissed like that before. Finally he released her.

"Oh God! I'm dreaming again." Kayla walked in circles, holding her head in her hands.

"You're plum goofy, lady."

"I think you said that already."

"Who told you I was dead?" He'd like to know the worm that was responsible for spreading that lie.

"I don't remember."

"Fine, If you do happen to remember let me know so that I can straighten the fellow out."

"Sure," she said, only half paying attention to him. Something was missing, she needed to remember what had happened to her.

She walked back into the little cabin. Kin was fiddling with something in the kitchen area. She pulled out a chair and sat down at the table.

"Are you hungry?" he asked her.

Kayla was a little hungry. She didn't think she'd eaten breakfast that morning.

"I could stand to eat."

"I hope you like beans and biscuits because it's really about all that I can cook."

"That would be just fine."

"And after supper I can boil some warm water for your bath, if you like."

"That would be nice."

Kin was feeling confused himself—one minute he wanted this crazy woman out of his house and then the next he didn't want her to go. He almost felt sorry for her.

Dinner was eaten in silence. Kayla and Kin exchanged nervous glances throughout the whole meal. He thought she was beautiful but she could be trouble. Kayla felt the same way: he was very handsome—but dangerous, she suspected.

"Are you finished eating?"

"Oh yes, it was very good, Kin, thank you."

"You're just being polite."

"No, it really was good," she insisted.

"I'm good at a lot of things." He winked at her. "But cooking isn't one of them."

Kayla put her head down, she just knew she was blushing again.

After Kin had cleared the dishes from the table he hauled in a large tub from outside.

"I usually bathe outside but it's still a little chilly out so you should bathe inside by the fire."

"I can't believe that you actually take a bath outside. Aren't you afraid that someone will see you?"

"Who's gonna see me?"

"Your neighbors, friends."

"The only person that ever comes around here is old Doc Price and hell, he's seen a hundred people wearing nothing but a silly grin."

"Really?" Kayla tried to keep from imagining Kin wearing nothing but a grin.

"Do you expect me to believe that you have never bathed outside?" he asked.

"Believe it or not, I prefer to stay indoors when I bathe."

"I like to kick back and look at the stars and the moon. Sometimes I wonder what it would be like to walk on the moon. Silly, isn't it?"

"It's not silly at all, maybe someday you can walk on the moon."

Kin laughed hysterically. "You say that like it could really happen."

"It has happened."

"Are you crazy? How would anyone get to the moon much less walk on it?" He shot her a dirty look.

"Oh, for Pete's sake, is my bath water ready yet?" she asked in frustration.

Kin added some cool water to the hot; it felt just right. He wouldn't want that silky-smooth skin to get burned, he wanted to touch her but—

"Do you mind?" she interrupted his thoughts. "I'd like to get undressed."

Kin stepped back and pulled shut a makeshift curtain so that she could have some privacy.

Kayla began to undress. Even though the curtain was between them she could feel his eyes on her. She found herself breathing heavier, she hoped that he couldn't hear her rapid breaths. He was so handsome, his eyes were the most amazing blue that she had ever seen and he smelled wonderful.

Kin knew that he should step outside, any decent man would,

but he just couldn't force himself to do so. He sat in his favorite chair and stared at the curtain. He could see her silhouette, he watched as she peeled her clothes off. The curtain didn't shield a whole lot; when she turned to the side to step into the tub he nearly bit off his tongue. She was thin, but not too thin, and her breasts were perky. His mouth started to get dry. God help him, he wanted this woman, he wanted her from the minute that he saw her on his doorstep, he wanted her with a passion that he could not escape, or explain, and it made him downright angry.

Kayla settled down into the warm water. "Kin, would you like to wash my back?" *What?* She couldn't believe that she just asked him that. Maybe he hadn't heard her.

He sat in silence, had he heard right? He wondered. Did she just ask if he wanted to wash her back?

"I can hear you breathing," she told him.

He wasn't breathing that loudly, was he? Maybe if he just sat quietly she would think that he had left the room. His heart raced.

"I know you're there, I can see your shadow, talk to me."

"What do you want me to say?"

"Do you want to wash my back?" *WHAT!* Was she an idiot? Did she really ask that again? First she asked Jake to make love to her and now she was asking a perfect stranger if he wanted to wash her back. She hadn't thought that she was desperate, but she sure was acting like it.

"Who washes your back at home?" he asked.

"I do."

"Then do it yourself now," he grumbled.

Kayla was at a loss for words. She just sat there, she was so embarrassed.

"I thought you said you weren't a whore."

"I am not a whore, Kin Parsons, and don't you dare call me one."

"If you're not a whore stop acting like one, only a whore would invite a strange man to wash her back."

Kayla could feel the hot tears coming. He was being so mean to her, but then, didn't she deserve it? He was right, how could she ask him that? He didn't feel like a stranger, he had spent the past few months in her head, in her dreams, she felt like she knew him. His words pulled her out of her thoughts.

"What if I had said yes?"

"What?"

"What if I had said yes, what if I had jerked that curtain back and stripped off my clothing and jumped right in that tub with you, what would you have done then?"

"I...I don't know," she stammered.

"I should take you in my arms and make love to you right now," he told her.

"That might not be so bad," she whispered to herself.

"I'm sure, Kayla, making love to you would be very satisfying but the truth is we barely know each other."

"I realize that, but I feel as if I have known you for a very long time."

"You should get out now, I still need a bath before the water gets cold."

Kayla stepped out of the tub and dried off in front of the fire that Kin had built a few hours earlier. It would need more wood soon, she noticed. Kayla saw the dried blood on her clothing, she didn't want to put it back on.

"Kin?"

"Yes."

"Would you by any chance have something for me to put on besides this bloody clothing?"

"I'm sure that I can find something." He disappeared and a few moments later returned with a large nightshirt that he handed to her over the curtain. She pulled it up over her head. It hung down to her ankles, but it was clean and that's all that mattered to her.

Kin took his turn in the bath. He had been in about five

minutes or so when he realized that the fire was dying down. He cursed softly.

"What's the matter?"

"I need some logs for the fire."

"I'll get them for you," she offered.

"The wood is on the back porch if you can carry it."

Kayla piled a few logs into her arms and carried them to the fireplace. She managed to avoid looking at him while she stoked the fire, she knew she would have to turn around eventually and then she would be forced to look at him. And when she did she couldn't help but stare at his broad, muscular chest. She had never seen such muscles on a man. He obviously worked hard, he had Jake beat on looks, she thought.

Kin watched as she studied him, their eyes met.

"Haven't you seen a naked man before?" He grinned.

"No… I mean yes, but not like you, you're so…big."

Kin looked down at his lap. "I didn't realize that you could see so well from that far away."

Kayla felt the blood rush to her face. "I meant that you have large muscles."

"One in particular." He looked down again.

"Excuse me?"

Maybe he shouldn't be teasing her; after all, it was obvious that she wanted him already.

Kayla looked down at her feet, wishing that she had polished her toenails. "I should let you finish your bath in peace. Do you have a hairbrush I could use?"

"In the other room, next to the wash basin."

"Thank you."

Kayla stood at the dresser. She caught her reflection in the handheld mirror that was propped up against the washbasin. She could see the color in her cheeks. Kin had probably seen it as well. By the way she had acted when she saw his bare chest he must think her an inexperienced child… No, he thought she was a whore, that's right, he had said it enough, just because she wore jeans and a tank top. The red in her cheeks was no longer an embarrassing blush, she was downright mad now. Besides, if he were so damn righteous he wouldn't have asked her to bring in the firewood where she could clearly see him half naked, and he wouldn't have talked to her the way that he did.

He was no better than she was, and she would tell him so, if he ever brought it up again.

"Kayla," he called out.

"What?" she snarled.

"You are going to stay the night, aren't you? It's dark outside and all, I think we should wait until morning to get you home."

"That's fine." He wasn't going to get an argument from her, not that she was looking forward to staying the night with him, or maybe she was. No, she was just tired and her head hurt. That was all.

"I'll make a pallet on the floor and you can sleep in the bed."

"Oh no, I'll sleep on the floor."

"I will not let an injured lady sleep on the floor, you're a guest. You will sleep in the bed," he insisted.

"I'm not hurt that bad and besides that I'm an uninvited guest... I will sleep on the floor." She didn't want to put him out any more than she already had.

Kin emerged from behind the curtain. He was wearing a pair of jeans but no shirt, his hair was wet and hanging down in his eyes. He reminded her of the stray dog that had been hanging around outside of her house a few weeks ago.

"You should get a haircut," she said without thinking.

"Are you offering to cut it?"

"No... Well...I suppose that I could cut it."

"I'll get the scissors." He jumped up from the fireplace and practically ran into the other room.

Kayla had never seen a man so happy about getting a haircut. She took his seat on the brick in front of the fire and warmed her cold feet. She thought about calling Shelly, but she didn't see a phone. It didn't surprise her not to see a phone, considering the fact that he had no indoor plumbing.

"I found them," he said, holding up a pair of rusty scissors for her to see. Only to Kayla it looked like a pair of rusty razor blades glued together.

"They don't look like they cut very well."

"Just do the best that you can, it couldn't possibly look any worse than it does now."

"That's true... I didn't mean that it looks bad, I...I just meant that it could stand to be out of your eyes." His eyes, they were so blue and beautiful.She could get lost in his eyes.

"So you won't be upset if I mess up?" she asked. Trying to get her mind off of his blue eyes, and his tan, muscular body.

"I don't get upset, I get even," he said in an intimidating way.

He sat down on the floor in front of her. Kayla cut several inches of his light brown hair. She didn't think it could be possible but he looked even more handsome now.

"All done," she said, handing him the scissors.

"I hope so, it doesn't feel like I have any hair left," he teased.

"You have plenty left." She pulled the towel from his shoulders and shook the hair from it. She brushed away what was on his bare shoulders, making him tingle at her touch. Kin picked up a handheld mirror to inspect her work; he nodded in approval.

"You did all right, but now it's your turn." He picked up the scissors and snapped them in her face.

"Over my dead body." She prepared to run.

"No, I won't kill you, but I'm not above sitting on you to keep you still while I chop off your locks." He flashed her a devilish grin.

"You wouldn't."

"I might." He winked.

"I would have to call the police on you."

"The who?"

"The police... You know, the law." Kayla rolled her eyes, this guy really didn't get out much. "Put down the scissors," she demanded, her face serious now.

"I woundn't cut off those beautiful locks even if you asked me to... But I would brush it for you, it looks to be a little tangled up."

Kayla's mother used to brush her hair for her when she was young. It had been a really long time ago.

"That would be nice, I'd like that."

Kayla sat between his legs while he brushed out her long, thick reddish locks.

"You have beautiful hair, and skin." Yes, he had said it, how could he not notice her beautiful skin when he was so close to her, it had been too long since he had been with a woman. He wasn't sure if he actually liked her, or just the thought of being with a woman again.

"Thank you, I try to stay out of the sun as much as possible." It was true. From the time she was young and got a horrible sunburn she had always been careful to put on plenty of sun screen and she always wore a hat while gardening.

"So what you're saying is you haven't done a lick of work in your life."

"I don't believe that's what I said, I just keep my skin covered when I am outside."

"I guess a whore doesn't get outside much in the first place, mostly all they do is lay on their backs." Now why in the hell did he go and say that? He didn't even know the answer to that himself. But he regretted it instantly. They had actually been getting along and he blew it.

"I'm not going to say this again, I am not a whore and I would like it very much if you would—"

"I was only joking this time, you are a feisty redhead, aren't you?"

"I'm only feisty when I need to be and my hair is not red."

"Yes, it is," he argued.

"Are you finished aggravating me yet? Because if you are I would like to get some sleep."

"It's just so much fun to aggravate you, Miss Kayla, but seeing that I have to get up when the rooster crows, we should both get some sleep now."

Kin helped Kayla get her pallet made and then he blew out the lantern as he left for his own bed. For the life of him he didn't know why but he wished that she would ask him to stay with her, to sleep beside her, to hold her, to make love to her. And if she had asked, he would have said yes.

Being alone had never really bothered him before, but tonight it was bothering him. She would never ask him to stay, not after the way he had accused her of being a whore all day. He must have called her that horrible name at least a half dozen times throughout the day. He knew full well that Kayla wasn't a whore, she was too pure for that. He found himself wondering if she had ever been with a man before. He would love to be her first.

But that was too good to be true, he was pretty sure that she was not a virgin, but he was also sure that it had been awhile since she'd felt the touch of a man.

He wouldn't blame her if she left in the middle of the night, but he hoped that she wouldn't, he actually looked forward to seeing her in the morning.

Kin took his clothes off and slipped in under the cool, crisp sheets. He preferred to sleep in the nude. He knew that he should wear a nightshirt with Kayla in the other room; however, she was wearing the only one that he owned.

Kin tossed and turned for what seemed like hours. He knew that he was not going to get any sleep, not as long as Kayla was under his roof.

He heard a noise, he strained to listen, it sounded as if she were talking to someone.

"Who the hell could she be talking to?" he asked himself.

Kin slipped out of bed and crept over to the doorway, where he had left Kayla. The firelight lit her face, she looked asleep, as he turned to go back to bed she suddenly jerked and whimpered, she must have been having a bad dream, he thought. He went to her side and gently shook her shoulders.

She didn't seem to realize he was there, she managed to kick off her covers, the nightshirt that he had loaned her was wrapped around her middle, Kin took in the sight of her long legs and her sheer white panties, he was starting to get aroused. What would she think if she awoke at that moment and found him standing over her nude and fully aroused? He scooted her over on the pallet, making room for himself beside her. He slid under the covers and put his arm around her middle and drifted off to sleep, a restful sleep, that is until Kayla clocked him in the chin with what he thought to be a very powerful right punch.

"What's the matter with you?" He grabbed her flailing fists before she could hit him again.

"Where am I?" She looked around the room, obviously confused.

Kin though that he was going to have to explain once again how he had found her on his doorstep, but her memory seemed to be coming back to her.

"I remember, I just wasn't fully awake yet."

"What were you dreaming about?"

"The same thing I aways dream about… You."

"I'm flattered."

"You came to me, told me that you were dead and that I could be next, then you just fell into my arms."

"As I told you before, I am not dead, I don't know why you keep insisting that I am, or that I'm going to be. It just upsets you, and honestly, it is starting to upset me as well."

"I can't control what I dream…and by the way, what are you doing in bed with me?"

"I could tell that you were having bad dreams so I didn't want you to be alone."

"So you just climbed into bed with me?" She pretended to be upset with him but she really wasn't.

"I just didn't want you to be alone, that's all."

She relaxed a little bit. "That's nice of you." She reached over and put her hand on his thigh, he grinned, and then she realized that he had an erection. She pulled her hand back.

"What the hell is that?" she asked.

"Well, if you don't know, sweetheart..."

"Oh, I know exactly what it is."

"That's too bad, I was hoping to teach you something."

Kayla pulled the covers back to reveal Kin in all his naked glory.

"What's that look about? "

"Why are you naked?"

"You have my only nightshirt."

"That's no excuse, all you had to do was put some pants on."

"I simply forgot to get dressed before I came to check on you, it was an honest mistake."

"Honest, do you really expect me to believe that nonsense?"

"I don't care if you believe it or not."

"You came in to console me, and maybe you thought that I would be so grateful that I would just let you make love to me."

"I thought no such thing... And have you forgotten that you are the one that dreams about me?"

"I have not forgotten that, and believe me, if I could change it I would, I'd love to erase you from my mind right this second," she spewed.

"You dream of making love to me and believe me, lady, your dreams can't come close to the real thing."

"A dream is a dream and I wouldn't dare let you touch me for real." She turned away from him.

"Who says I would want to? Maybe I should just go back to my own room."

"Yes, you should."

Kin stood up, still partially aroused and in no way trying to hide his nakedness. He figured that it would serve her right to see what she had passed up on. She stared in awe of him, he was so perfectly proportioned, and yes she did want him to touch her, she wanted that more than anything, but she wouldn't give in to it, not now, not yet anyway.

She laid her head back on the pillow and sighed, she knew that she couldn't get back to sleep now, but she closed her eyes anyway. Suddenly she cought a glimsp of a man in her mind , she was not dreaming this time, it was a memory, like a flashback. The man stood in front of her, he was angry, he was yelling at her, she got the feeling that he wanted to kill her. It was all she could stand, she opened her eyes and jumped up from the pallet, she busted through the door of Kin's room.

"Is there something I can help you with?" he asked in a cool tone.

"I remembered something."

Kin sat up in bed, she was upset again, he knew that he shouldn't care, but he couldn't help himself. "What is it, honey?"

"I remember a man, I think he may have been one of my ranch hands."

"Sit with me." He patted the side of the bed, urging her to sit beside him. "I want you to tell me everything that you can remember."

Kayla climbed up on the large bed beside Kin, he held her hand tenderly. "Okay, I was standing on the top of the hill behind my house, I was looking for rocks to border my flowerbed, there was one particular rock that caught my interest… Oh God, no…"

"What is it?" Now he was really concerned about her, what on earth upset her so much?

"The rock… It has your name on it."

"Anyone could have put their name on that rock. I'm sure others have the same name as I have."

"No, it's your name. I remember he told me Kin Parsons was buried in that spot over a hundred years ago and his family had killed you for stealing the ranch from him."

Kin rubbed his hands over his face, was she a nut? Or did she truly believe this to be real?

"I think I look pretty good to over be a hundred years old, don't you think?"

"This is no time to joke."

"I don't mean to upset you even more, but put yourself in my place, what if I were telling you these things?"

"I guess you're right, you must think I'm crazy, maybe I am. I wish Shelly were here."

"Who is Shelly?"

"She is my best friend, I can tell her anything and she always makes me feel better, she is probably worried about me."

"I'll take you to her in the morning."

"I'd like to call her right now, if you have a phone that is."

"I don't have a phone, but I will take you to your friend when the sun comes up." He had no clue what a phone was; he didn't want to get into it either, not after all her crazy talk of running water and inside toilets. Her voice brought him out of his thoughts.

"What year are you living in anyway?"

"What?" She caught him off guard. "I would imagine the same year you are living in."

"Humor me."

"It's 1876, right?"

"No, it's 2007," she said numbly.

"That's impossible."

"No, it isn't, it's 2007," she insisted.

"I believe you think that it is, but, my dear, there is no way that we are living in two different years."

"Kin, I was born in 1969, and that was the same year that a man walked on the moon."

"I don't believe it, I won't believe it."

"I have heard people talk of time travel but I never really believed it could happen."

"That's because it can't, it's not possible."

"It is possible, I have done it, I don't know how I did it but I did." She looked at him in amazement.

"So you're telling me that someone really has walked on the moon?"

"Yes, it has been done, Kin, I promise you I am not fabricating this, if you can take me home I'll prove it to you."

"I'll take you home if you can take me to the moon," he snickered.

"I wish I could, it's not that easy."

"The sun is up now, get dressed and I will take you home." Kin had to get this woman home, she was a nutcase, how could he be so damn attracted to someone who was obviously this looney?

By the time that Kin had gotten dressed and outside Kayla had been out looking around the property, it was so familiar to her.

"I don't see any cars, how are you going to take me home?"

"I don't know what a car is, do you still have horses in your day?"

"I haven't been on a horse in years," she admitted.

"Well, you're fixin to get reacquainted with one." He saddled up two horses. "This one is yours, her name is Girda, she'll go easy on you."

As they rode Kayla took in the scenery. Parts of it looked familiar, but she didn't see a paved rode anywhere; it felt as if they had ridden for hours, when Kin finally broke the silence.

"This is town."

Kayla looked around, it was a pitiful sight. "This isn't McAlester, it couldn't be."

"Yes, it is."

Kayla saw three buildings to the left of the road and five to the right, they all looked as if a strong wind could knock them down. There was a saloon ,a woman was standing in the doorway, giving Kin a come-hither look.

"I declare, if it ain't Kinny Parsons"

"Mornin', Maggie." He tipped his hat in her direction.

"Lookin' for a goot time, sweetie?"

"Not today, Maggs, maybe next time."

"Come on now, you know I do things no other can." She looked directly at Kayla and smiled.

"I'm sure you could, Maggs, not today."

"Well, you know where to find me." She retreated back ito the saloon.

"So, how often do you come into town?"

"Usually once a month, just to get supplies."

"Is that all you come for, supplies?" she asked with a hint of jelousy in her voice.

"Don't tell me you're jealous of Maggs."

"Of course not, what you do, and who you do it with, is none of my business."

"If it matters, I have never paid for the services of a woman. As a matter of fact, it was not long ago I had a woman, we were to be married."

Kayla was curious to know what kind of woman would let a man like this get away.

"What happened?"

"She decided that she would rather have a man's money than a man's love."

"She was a fool."

Kin stopped his horse and looked at Kayla. "She was not a fool, she just fell for the wrong man." Why was he defending her? She did, after all, break his heart.

"I didn't mean any disrespect, but she would have to be a fool to let you go."

"Whatever, so now what do we do?"

"I don't know, none of this looks familiar."

If there had been any doubts earlier there were none now, she was stuck in the year 1876 and she had no clue how to get home.

"I don't know how to get home, Kin, I guess we just go back to your place, if that's okay with you." She wanted to get home but until she figured out a way to do it she was stuck there, with Kin. She had to make the best of it.

Kin thought. He knew that it wasn't a good idea for him to take her back with him but hell, what was he gonna do, leave her out there alone? She had nowhere to go and knew no one.

"Okay, let's go back to the cabin," he told her.

"Yes, my backside has had enough of Girda for one day, no offense, girl." She patted the horse on her neck. Girda neighed as if to say no offense taken. Kayla rubbed her aching behind.

"That's a fine backside you have there, little lady."

Kayla's head snapped around to see one of the ugliest men she had ever seen.

"What do you want, Pete?" Kin asked the man.

"Ain't you gonna introduce me to the lady?"

"No," he stated plainly. The horses fidgeted in the street, the man made them nervous.

Kayla knew that animals could sense danger and she even sensed that this man was dangerous.

"Fine, I'll get straight to the point, when you gonna sell your land?"

"Never."

Kayla saw two other men approach. They stopped their horses right in the path of them so that they could not leave. Kayla shifted uncomfortably in her saddle.

Kin knew all about these men and what they were capable of. They had been in trouble with the law for stealing cattle and who knows what else. He needed to get Kayla away from them as soon as possible.

"Tell your goon brothers to get out of my way."

"I ain't through talkin' to you yet."

"I'm through talkin' to you, you're not getting my land, you'll have to kill me first."

"That can be arranged," Pete said, spitting a wad of nastly black chewing tobacco at the hoof of Kin's horse.

The other two moved away so that they could pass. As they rode off Pete called out to her, "If you ever want a real man call me, sweetheart." It made the hair on her neck stand up. Kin was silent on most of the ride home.

"He threatened your life, for your land, you act like it was nothing."

"It is nothing, just let it go," he told her.

"Aren't you afraid that he will act on it someday?"

"I won't live my life being afraid of Pete and his brothers."

The closer they got to Kin's property the more Kayla recognized, it was home, her home. If she were right she knew that somewhere in a nearby clump of trees she would find an oak with initials carved in it. She stopped Girda and stared at the hillside and the group of trees at the top.

"Don't stop now, we are almost to the barn."

"This is my land," she told him.

"What? Now you want my land too?"

"No, I mean this is my land in the future."

"I don't think so."

"I realize that you own it now, but in 2007 I own it."

"Are you still on that time travel idea? There is just no way possible that can happen."

"I can prove it."

"How's that?"

"Over in that clump of trees there is one that has a set of initials carved into it."

"What does that prove?"

"When I was younger I used to pretend that my boyfriend and I had put our initials in that tree."

"I still don't get how it proves you traveled through time."

"Did I hit a sore spot with the tree and initial thing?"

Kin unsaddled the horses and started to cool them down. He ignored her question so she decided to find the tree on her own. She walked quickly up the hill, checking every one until she found the one she was looking for. She ran her hand across the deep cuts in the trunk.

"Did you find what you were looking for?" Kayla jumped, Kin had come up behind her undetected.

"Yes, what was her name?" she asked, once again tracing the deep grooves of the initials K.P. loves K.H.

"Her name was...is Kelly Hall."

"You must have loved her very much."

"I did,but that was awhile ago. I think about her at times, but I don't love her any longer."

"Do you believe me now, how else would I know about this tree?"

"Apparently you have seen it before, you were snooping around out here this morning, how do I know you didn't see it then."

"What would I have to gain by lying?"

"I don't know, Kayla , I'm tired of playing your games." He started back to the cabin.

"I'm not playing games, this is my home." She stomped her feet in the dirt.

"If you did travel through time to get here then just travel back and go home, I'm sick of looking at you and I'm sick of listening to you."

Kayla raced past him to reach the cabin first, she pulled off the shirt that Kin had loaned her and tossed it to the floor. Pulling her tank top back over her head, she began to cry.

"Thank you for the food and the bed last night, I won't bother you again." She walked past him and damn herself she almost wished that he would stop her.

"My pleasure, have a nice evening." He tipped his hat to her and let the door slam behind her, the glass rattling in the windows.

Kayla looked back at the cabin, what would she do now? Where would she go? The last time she had felt this lost was when her parents had died. She had to find her way home.

Kayla went to the stables; maybe she could sleep there for the night and then in the morning she would try to figure out a way to get home.

As she opened the barn door she could feel all eyes on her.

"Don't worry, fellas, I won't hurt you, I just need a place to lay my aching head for the night ."

The horses neighed as if they understood what she was saying and they went back to eating their oats, since he had already fed and watered the animals she knew that Kin would not be back to the barn that night.

She found some blankets by the wall and curled up on a stack of hay, in no time she was asleep. For the first time in months Kayla had a deep, peaceful and dreamless sleep.

FIVE

Kin had been tossing and turning all night long. He cursed himself for not chasing after Kayla. He wondered where she had spent the night, who she spent it with, was she cold? Was she hungry?

He dressed for his usual day of work on the ranch; he found himself hoping that Kayla would return. Why? He couldn't answer that question, as nutty as she was he couldn't help but like her even though he should have been happy to be rid of her. He fried up some bacon and biscuits for breakfast; he then put on a pot of water to boil. By the time he returned from the barn his water would be good and hot. Hot coffee was just what he needed after his sleepless night. Since Kayla had distracted him and taken up his whole day he had got nothing done so today he would have to make up for it. He really needed to repair a broken fence before he lost his entire herd of cattle.

When Kin reached the barn he knew instantly that something was different, someone was inside. He cracked the door open carefully with his knife in his hand, ready to attack if need be; after all, it was just yesterday that his life had been threatened. What he saw in the barn was not life threatening. Kayla was fast asleep on a hay pile with the horse blankets wrapped around her; she was so beautiful, he thought.

Kin pulled the door shut and started for the outhouse. He made sure to yell to his horse, he knew that Kayla would not want him to know that she had slept in his barn.

"Wake up. Steel, we gotta lot of work to do," he spoke loudly.

At the sound of his voice Kayla woke. She quickly put the blanket back on the hook where she had found it. She rearranged the hay so that the imprint of her body no longer showed. She peeked out the barn door just in time to see Kin disappear inside the outhouse. He was watching her from a hole in the wood; he watched her duck inside the cabin.

She was taken aback by the wonderful aroma of fried bacon and fresh biscuits, she was famished, surely he wouldn't notice a few slices missing, and a biscuit or two. It was so delicious, she let out a loud burp, she looked around and giggled, she was glad she was alone, that hadn't been very ladylike. She wondered if this was how she was going to spend the rest of her life, sneaking around, stealing food and sleeping in strange barns. She could get a job, but who was going to hire a crazy woman from the future?

Kayla roamed around the cabin. She stopped in front of the big tub, her memory reverting back to the night before when Kin had bathed, the bubbles from the soap surrounding his muscular body. Maybe she could get used to living in this time, she thought. Who was she kidding? She had been born into a world with electricity, running water, television. She really liked not having to leave the house to use the bathroom. She couldn't even find a damn clock in this cabin, how would she even know what time it was? Not that it really mattered.

Kayla heard horses approaching. She carefully pulled back the curtain and peered outside the window. She could see that creepy guy Pete from yesterday and his two goon brothers were right behind him. A chill went up her spine as she remembered the threats that they had made against Kin. They jumped off of their horses and headed for the cabin.

Kayla looked around for a place to hide but she wasn't fast enough. The door burst open and Pete stood before her chewing that same nasty black tobacco. He spat a wad onto the floor and gave her a silly grin.

"Well, what have we got here?"

"It's that gal from yesterday, Pete," said one of the other men.

"I know that, Teddy, you idiot." Pete smacked Teddy upside the head.

"Well, if you knowed why'd you ask for?"

Kayla rolled her eyes at the idiots who stood before her; by the way they spoke they obviously hadn't made it past the third grade, and by the way they smelled they probably hadn't bathed for that long either.

"Shut up," Pete barked at his brother.

"I didn't know you was stayin' here with ol' Kinny boy." He stepped closer to her, making her very uncomfortable.

"I-I'm not," she stammered. "I was actually just leaving." She tried to walk past the men but they blocked her, refusing to let her by.

Pete put his arm around her waist and pulled her body up against his. "Not so fast, missy, you ain't goin' nowhere." The stench of his rotten breath almost made her pass out but she pulled herself together.

"My name is not Missy and would you please turn me loose?" She was trying to act tough but the honest truth was she was terrified of these men and what they might do to her.

The third man stood in the doorway, watching and waiting for his chance to speak. "You sure got a mouth on you," he finally spoke.

"Well, what do you know, it speaks."

The third man crossed the room to stand before her, he then slapped her so hard across the face that it made her bite her tongue, she swallowed hard, tasting blood.

"Damn, Bob, you didn't have to do that," Pete told him.

74

Now she knew the bastard's name, the third brother was named Bob, he was tall and ugly, even though Pete did most of the talking she had a feeling that this Bob was the leader, he seemed to be the only one with half a brain.

"You got a big mouth, lady, and you should learn when to shut it, or someone will shut it for you."

"How dare you—"

"I said shut up, you little whore, before I shut you up for good." He had his hand poised to slap her again and she knew she had better not push him too far or he would kill her, there was no doubt in her mind that he was capable of killing her. But yet she couldn't stop herself from speaking.

"I am not a whore," she spat back at him. She didn't know why it was so but all the men in this time seemed to like calling her a whore.

"Maybe you're not one now, but when me and the boys get done with you..."

Kayla's eyes grew large.

"Oh boy, Bob, can I go first this time?" asked Teddy.

"We'll talk about it later, first things first, where is the man of the house?" Bob asked.

"I don't know. I told you I was about to leave." She tried to get past them again, to no avail.

"I don't think so, ya see, the three of us, we stayed up all night makin' plans for you and ol' Kinny boy."

"That's right, we got plans fer ya," Teddy chimmed in.

"Shut up, Teddy," the other two men said in unison.

"Look, I don't know what plans you idiots think you have but I have plans of my own and they do not include the three of you. So if you will move out of my way, I'll be leaving now."

Pete stepped aside, allowing her to pass him. The tobacco smell was overwhelming. As she neared the doorway she actually thought she might have a chance to escape. She saw Kin riding up to the cabin. She ran out the door, wanting to throw herself in his arms.

SHARON HENDRYX MCDANIEL

He was off the horse before the animal had even come to a stop. He pulled Kayla close to him and held her as if she belonged to him.

"What are you doing on my land?" he demanded to know.

"As I was telling your lady friend, me an' the boys have been up all night making plans for the two of you."

"Well, I'm changing your plans, whatever they are: get off my property and leave us alone."

"I don't think so," said Bob. "We came to do something and we are gonna finish what we started."

Kin stood face to face with Bob now. "I said leave this property now."

"Oh, we will leave but your little whore will be going with us." Bob grabbed Kayla and pulled her away from Kin. He pulled her back, it was like a game of tug of war that neither of the men intended on losing.

"You'll have to kill me before I let you take her." Kin looked deep into Kayla's eyes.

As if he were trying to tell her something.

"Well now, haven't we been tellin you fer years that one day we was gonna kill you?"

"Yep, been tellin' fer years," Teddy repeated.

Bob paced the ground back and forth in front of them. "We offered to buy this land, but you wouldn't sell it, so now we are just gonna take it, and the lady is a bonus we didn't plan on, but we will have fun with her. We need another woman around the house, right, Pete?"

"Yep, them whores in town cost too much, we need one of our very own."

Kin started to walk back towards the cabin, holding Kayla's hand tightly, pulling her along. He knew they were in a bad postion and he wasn't sure if he could get them out of it.

"Remember yesterday when you said we could have your land over your dead body?" Bob asked.

Kin and Kayla both turned around to see Bob holding his pistol aimed right at Kin.

"That's just what we plan on doin."

"I'll give you the land and everything else, just let me and the lady walk away together, right now," he pleaded with Bob.

"No, it's too late to make deals, you're gonna die and your whore will be my whore, we gonna have fun tonight, ain't we, boys?"

"Yeee haaaa."

"Can I go first?" Teddy asked again.

Kayla had heard him ask that once already but it hadn't sank in until now what he meant by that—they were going to rape her and he wanted to be first. She felt sick. She'd sooner die before she let these pigs touch her.

"We'll talk about it later, Teddy, first we gotta get rid of this here coyboy." Pete approached Kayla and traced her face with his rough hand. She turned away from him.

Kin made a move for Pete and told Kayla to run. She tried but Teddy grabbed her and the next thing she knew Kin and Bob were involved in a fistfight. It looked like Kin was getting the best of Bob. Pete joined in to help his brother. When Teddy loosened his grip she kneed him in the groin and he let go of her. She ran for Kin. Just as she reached him there was a loud bang, it was a gunshot. Pete stood behind Kin with a look in his eyes that she couldn't begin to describe. Kin fell to the floor. Pete had shot him in the back.

Kayla's worst fears coming true, this was what she had been dreaming about. The man she could have loved, she would never get the chance to know. She held his head in her lap, silently crying for the man she was supposed to have loved, fate was cruel.

Bob pulled her to her feet and dragged her out of the cabin, they stood outside for a few minutes, she tried to get loose but Bob's grip was too tight, she could do nothing but watch as Pete lit a match and the cabin burst into flames, leaving Kin's body to be burned.

The three men laughed wildly as they mounted their horses. "Our work here is done," said Bob. "Let's go home."

Kayla was stuck riding with Teddy, the foulest-smelling of the bunch, just her rotten luck. She knew that it was only a matter of time before Pete and Bob gave him permission to have his way with her. She knew she had to get away before that happened. She almost felt guilty for thinking about trying to save herself when Kin had just been murdered and set on fire, but she had to escape these creeps; without Kin there would be no one else to save her, so she just had to save herself.

As the cabin burned around him, he opened his eyes, at first he thought he'd died and gone to hell, but he wasn't dead, not yet anyway. He rolled onto his belly and crawled slowly through the smoke, he could hear the wood cracking around him, he barely made it outside before the roof came down.

"What the hell happened?" hHe asked himself. Then he remembered, them nasty old Reed boys, they tried to make good on their threat to kill him, they tried, but they hadn't succeeded, at least not yet. He was down but he wasn't out. He didn't plan on giving them the satisfaction of seeing him dead. Something else crossed his mind—*Did they kill Kayla?*

Or did they take her with them? Even though he hurt like hell and could barely get around Kin knew that he was going to survive his wound, he had to find Kayla but he couldn't do it alone. Now he knew all too well what these creeps were capable of and he had to save this poor girl, the poor girl who believed that she was from the future. He couldn't stand the thought of them with their dirty hands all over her, possibly even killing her once they had gotten what they wanted from her.

Kin crawled his way to the barn. His horse Steel was waiting for him, the horse knew that something bad was wrong when he saw his owner doubled over in pain. Kin fell onto the hay stack that Kayla had slept on the night before. He could still smell a hint of the lavender soap that she had bathed with.

Steel pressed his cold nose to his owner, probably the only thing keeping him from passing out. He mustered all the strength he could and climbed onto the horse's back.

"Take me to Doc's," he told him. He looked back one last time, the cabin had been a burning ball but now it was just a little flame, nothing left but ashes.

As Steel took him where he needed to go Kin had been thinking about Kayla and her dream. It had been a premonition, she was so sure that it would come true and it did, somewhat, she thought he would die but he didn't. And he had no intention on letting that part of her dream come true. If anyone was going to die it would be those Reed brothers, as soon as he was capable of taking care of them.

As he rode on he felt himself become weaker, slowly he slid off the saddle and onto the ground with a thud. The horse looked at him with sadness in his big brown eyes.

"You have to go for help, boy, I need you to bring Doc here."

To others Steel was just a horse, another animal, but Kin and even Doc Price knew that he was more than that, he was as smart as any person could be—actually, smarter than most people. He'd saved Kin's skin before and he had no doubt that he would save him again.

The town was bustling with people who were in doing their monthly shopping, no one seemed to notice the riderless horse, that was until Steel trotted directly into the saloon.

The barkeep did a double take.

"Someone get that beast out of my saloon before I shoot it," he barreled.

Doc looked up from his whiskey glass and smiled. He led the horse outside.

"Where is Kinny?" he asked, looking across the street expecting to see his old friend.

The horse pranced around a bit and then ran in circles around the old man.

"Okay, I get the hint, something has happened to our friend,and it can't be good." He hopped onto the horse and let him lead the way.

Steel raced to where he had left his owner. Doc thought he might fall off before they got there, he found himself wishing he hadn't swallowed so much whiskey—it was starting to sour in his belly. Hell, he might need a doctor before it was all over.

They found Kin passed out on the ground in the spot where Steel had left him, there was blood everywhere, he was very weak.

"Wake up,boy." Doc slapped him around a bit.

Kin opened his eyes and gave Doc a tiny grin. "I knew Steel would find you…in the saloon, I'm guessing."

"Yep, now shut up and try to help me get you on this here animal, fast. We need to get you to my cabin."

"Mine burned down," he whispered.

"Hellfire, son, just as soon as I get you sewed up you're gonna have to tell me about it."

"I gotta bullet in my back."

"I can see that much. I bet somewhere there is a woman in this story."

"She's beautiful."

"She had better be, to go through this kind of trouble."

They arrived at Doc's house just as the sun was going down. Doc barely managed to get Kin hoisted into his bed.

"Roll over and let me have a look."

A few minutes passed before Kin finally asked if Doc could get the bullet out.

"I can try." Doc reached for a bottle of whiskey. "Drink up, boy, it's all I've got for the pain."

Doc dug the bullet out and doctored him up the best he could, he sat beside his friend for hours on end, this boy was almost like his own son, he wouldn't be able to stand it if he didn't make it through this. But the way he saw it, he could only do the best he could to fix him, it was up to the good Lord to decide who lived and who died. Several days had passed before Kin finally opened his eyes.

"Am I still alive?" he asked Doc.

"Oh, you're alive, thanks to me, that horse of yours, and the good Lord, but no thanks to that woman who put you in danger in the first place."

"She didn't cause this, matter of fact, she tried to warn me of it, she knew I was in trouble but I just wouldn't listen to her. She said she dreamed I was going to die, she came to warn me. I didn't believe a word she said until it was too late."

"Sounds like a bunch of hooey to me, she didn't have no dream, she must have known all along. Dreamed it my butt, who did put that bullet in you son?"

"Pete Reed, they been saying they would put a bullet in me if I didn't surrender my land."

"And they finally done it to you, didn't they?"

"Yep. It came to that point, never thought they'd go through with it."

"Why didn't you just walk away?" Doc asked.

"I tried, I told them they could have it all if they just let me and the woman leave, they said it was too late to bargain and the next thing I knew I was crawling out of a burning cabin."

"I'm guessing they took the woman with them."

"They think I'm dead, they shot me and left me to burn in that cabin, they took Kayla and I gotta find her, Doc…before they do something terrible to her." He tried to get up.

Doc gently pushed him back down on the bed. "You're not going anywhere, son."

"Look, Doc, I know I just met this woman a day ago but I think that I love her."

"It's been more than a day, son, you've been out in my bed for three days now."

"Three days, there's no telling what those scoundrels have done to that poor girl, if she's still alive, I have to find her, Doc." He tried to get up again but he just didn't have the strength.

"You'll do no such thing, Kin, if she means that much to you, then I'll just have to find her myself."

"I can't let you do that, Doc, this is my fight, they started it but I have to be the one to finish it."

"You haven't got a choice, son, you're in no condition to get out of that bed much less be in a fight, besides, this might be the last adventure this old man gets to go on. The last chance to rescue a lady in need."

"Are you sure, Doc?"

"I'm sure, you'd just better stay in this bed and heal up."

"I promise." After all, what could he do? Those few seconds he had sat up hurt so bad he thought he might pass out from it, he knew there was no way he could ride a horse in this condition. And he'd definitely lose any fights he was to get into. That wouldn't do him or Kayla any good.

SIX

By the time the Reeds had reached their own ranch Kayla was exhausted, she just didn't care what happened to her any longer; she didn't know how to get home to her friends and her own time, she had lost the only one she knew in this time and quite possibly the only man she might ever be able to love in her lifetime.If she fell off the stupid horse and was trampled to death at that very moment she wouldn't have cared.

The horses stopped outside of this run-down shack that didn't even look livable to her.

"Teddy, give the horses some water and put them in the barn for the night," Bob ordered.

Pete and Bob grabbed Kayla by the arms and led her to a different run-down shack, this one was behind the barn. A feeling of dread hit her, could this be the end for her?

She wondered. Strange, it was only a few minutes ago that she cared less if she lived or died but now she was ready to fight for her life. She knew that she had to get away from those men. She would have to find her way home or die trying. She would have to make a run for it, there was nothing as far as she could see but being eaten by coyotes would be better than what the Reeds had planned for her. She took one more look at her surroundings before they pushed her inside the building, slamming the door shut behind her. She could hear hammering on the outside of the door, they weren't taking any chances on her getting away. She heard something scurry around her feet, she hoped it wasn't mice, she hated mice.

It was dusk, what little light there was coming through the slats of the walls would soon be gone. She moved about the small room, there was a table with two chairs and in one corner was a small cot with a pillow and a blanket. Kayla plopped down on the cot, the dust that stirred up made her sneeze, but sneezing was the least of her problems, she put her head down just to rest for a moment, she didn't want to fall asleep but before she could help herself she was in a deep slumber. She dreamt about Kin, she could see his handsome face so clearly, as if he were standing before her, alive and well. He held his hand out to her and she took it.

"I'm alive because of you," he told her. And then he took her into his arms and gave her the longest, most wonderful kiss.

"Wake up," she heard someone whisper.

Kayla struggled to open her eyes, she couldn't wait to see Kin's face. What she saw instead made her feel ill: she stared into the fat red face of Teddy Reed. He was standing over her and his hand was under her blouse, touching her bare skin. He squeezed her left breast. She slapped him so hard her hand stung.

"Why'd you do that for?" he asked stupidly.

"Because you don't just touch a woman like that."

"Can I touch you?" he asked stupidly.

"No, you cannot touch me." She could tell her answer made him angry.

"It don't matter what you say, whore, I'll do what I want anyway."

"No, you won't, you're not going to lay one filthy finger on me, you beast."

"I'm gonna lay all my fingers on you, and you're gonna like it," he insisted.

He inched towards her, her only hope for escape would be to overpower him and by the size of him it wasn't looking like an option.

Teddy reached out and ran his fingers through her hair. She closed her eyes and said a prayer.

"Teddy, get away from her." Pete to the rescue.

Thank you, Pete. However, it didn't make her feel any better; actually, Pete was worse than Teddy and if he stopped Teddy from molesting her it was only because he wanted to do it himself.

"You know I'm first in line," Pete told him.

"You always get to go first, it's my turn."

Kayla watched as they fought back and forth, the fight got so intense they seemed to forget that she was even there. As they inched away from the door she saw her opportunity for escape, she slid along the wall, getting closer and closer to sweet freedom.

She could smell the fresh air, one foot out the door and then the other, as she turned to run she smacked right into the third brother. Bob stood so firm that when she ran into him it knocked her to the ground with a thud.

"Hey, you chuckle heads, get out here." Bob picked Kayla up by the wrist and pulled her to her feet.

"You're not leaving yet, missy. As a matter of fact, you're not ever leaving, this is your new home so you might as well get used to it," he told her.

The two goons emerged from the shack.

"You almost let her get away, Teddy," Pete accused, trying to put the blame on his brother. She hated them all but still there was a very small part of her that felt sorry for the way Teddy got treated by his brothers.

"I want her while there's still some fight in her," Pete told Bob.

"I gotta a feelin this one has plenty of fight in her. And no one touches her until I say so."

"Okay, Bob." Teddy put his head down and pouted like a child who had just been denied his favorite candy.

Pete, on the other hand, spit a wad of his favorite tobacco and gave Kayla a look that she would never forget. It chilled her to the bone, the man was pure evil and he wasn't going to be satified until he had his way with her.

"Sit down," Bob ordered Kayla. She obeyed.

"I'm keeping you here until I decide what's best."

"I think it best if you let me go home."

"Your home is wherever I am."

"What are you saying?"

"I'm saying that I will make you my wife, at least that's what I'm thinking right now."

"I will not marry the likes of you, and you cannot force me," she said defiantly.

Bob came to her, grabbing her face in his hands, kissing her hard on the mouth. He tore at her blouse, trying to rip it off. She slapped and kicked with all her might but to no avail, all she managed to do was exhaust herself. She wilted into a heap on the cot. Bob finally managed to rip off her tank top and he cupped her breasts in his big rough hands. One hand dropped to her pants, where he managed one handed to undo her jeans.

"A lady don't need to be wearing these britches." He ripped them from her body.

As he caressed her legs, Kayla flinched. Was this how it was going to happen? He would have his way with her and then he'd let his brothers in on the action. How did she end up in this predicament, she wondered, would she ever get home?

Just when she thought it was a done deal Bob pulled away and tossed a dress at her. "Put this on," he ordered.

She did as she was told.

"Sit down and eat," he told her.

What? When did he bring food in? She looked to the table to find a bowl of what looked like stew, and some bread. Someone had obviously come in when she had her eyes closed, thinking she was going to be raped.

"I bet Kinny will be rolling in his grave when he finds out I have his land…and his woman."

"You're not going to have me."

"Woman….shut your trap. I'm running this show and you'd better learn your place."

Kayla plopped down at the little table and ate the slop that had been set for her. She almost hoped he had poisoned it so that she wouldn't have to worry about escaping anymore. She knew that her only escape would be to get Teddy alone, he was so dumb surely she could get away from him.

Doc had ridden to Kin's land to have a look around. The cabin was gone, burnt to the ground. He shook his head from side to side in disbelief. It was a shame, those Reed men had been getting away with raping and pillaging for years, it was time someone put a stop to it. But Doc was just an old man, not much chance that he could do anything to stop them, at least not alone, and Kin was in no condition to even get out of bed. The best thing for Doc to do was make Kin stay in bed, heal up and get out of town, it would be best if the Reed boys thought Kin was really dead.

Doc had an idea. He went up to the top of the hill, he found a large rock, he disturbed the ground enough to make it look like someone had been digging there. He wanted the Reeds to think that someone had come along, found Kin's remains and buried him. He pulled out a knife and scratched and scratched until Kin's name was clearly etched on the surface. The only peace he had right then was knowing that the grave was empty, but the Reeds wouldn't know that because they would be too stupid to look. He hoped that boy was staying in bed like he had ordered him to, he didn't need to be off looking for that woman he was so crazy about, if he had to guess Doc figured that the Reeds had already done their damage to her, he'd be lucky to find her alive. Doc had seen many women who had experienced the wrath of the Reeds and most were never the same afterwards.

Kayla listened closely, she could hear the men coming closer, their speech was slurred, it sounded as if they'd been drinking.

"Don't go near that shack," she heard Bob warn.

Shortly after she heard the warning the door opened and she saw Pete's ugly face grinning back at her, it looked like he had been in another fight, and lost.

"Bob ain't gonna help you now," he told her. "What did you do to him?" she asked.

"I didn't force him to drink all that whiskey, he done it to himself, he'll be out awhile."

"What?"

"He passed out… Figure till morning."

It wasn't even getting dark yet, she noticed. It would be hours until sundown.

Pete closed the gap between them. She closed her eyes, knowing that this was it, she had escaped them too long, Bob wasn't going to save her from Pete this time. She heard glass break, when she opened her eyes she saw Teddy standing over Pete with a broken bottle. Pete was splayed out on the ground, completely unconscious.

"Oh, Teddy, thank you," she said. It was time to do some acting, she hoped what little acting she had done in high school drama class would help her out now, this might be her only chance for escape with two of them passed out.

She took Teddy by the hand led him to the cot.

"I'm so glad you came back to me, I've been waiting for you." She almost choked on her own words.

"I'm back," was all he could manage to spit out.

Kayla wiggled against him, managing to get his gun, she kept it behind her back. Until Teddy tried to kiss her. She pulled the gun out from behind her back and pointed it at him, she cocked it to let him know that she meant business. She really didn't want to shoot the goofy bastard, but she would if she had to.

"Sit on the cot," she ordered.

"No."

"I mean it, Teddy, I'll shoot you dead just like Pete did to Kin, now sit on the cot."

"You ain't gonna shoot me, I bet you can't even aim that thing," he taunted.

Kayla pointed the gun at Teddy's left foot and pulled the trigger, just barely missing his toes. He jumped up on the cot and let out a loud yelp.

"You almost took my foot off, you little whore."

"If you call me a whore one more time the next shot won't miss."

"Whore."

Bang!

"You shot me, ya really shot me."

"Stop your whining, I warned you, didn't I?" She couldn't stand a whiner.

Kayla started for the door, she was getting the hell out of there before one of the others came out of their liquor-induced comas.

"Ya can't just leave me here to die."

"Shut up, you aren't going to bleed to death, and I'm going home."

"Where's home? We killed your old man."

"It's none of your business where home is to me, it's far away from here, and that's all that matters."

Kayla put some fruit in a bag and a canteen of water around her neck. "I'm going to lock you in here."

"Please don't lock me in," he begged.

"I said please but it didn't stop you from locking me in here."

"I'm scared," he whimpered.

"I don't really care, Teddy, I'm out of here."

"But Bob and Pete... They will kill me when they wake up."

"I can't help that, you're on your own now." Kayla slammed the door and put the board up against it to lock Teddy in the same way that they had locked her in. She wished it had been ol' Pete she shot in the foot. She checked the gun and saw it was empty, useless to her now. She tossed it to the ground and headed for the barn. She saddled up the smallest horse she could find, maybe it wasn't the smartest choice but it would be easier for her to get on and off of the smaller one. She led the polka-dotted mare out of the barn and climbed on her back. She pat her head and gave her a little pep talk before they started off. Kayla looked back to make sure that no one was following her. She caught a glimpse of a woman in the doorway of the cabin, their eyes met briefly before the woman put her hands around her protruding belly. It was as if to tell Kayla to run for her life before she ended up the same way. She couldn't imagine having the offspring of one of the Reeds. The lady put a hand up and waved Kayla on.

She was wasting too much time; she needed to get going. She knew she needed to get far away but she wanted to find Kin's place, she had to see for herself how badly the cabin had burned. Was there anything left of it? Was there anything left of Kin?

The sun beat down on her pale skin. It wouldn't be long before it started to set. She would need to find somewhere to sleep, she had no lantern, no matches, it would get cold at night without a fire. For every thought she started her mind always wandered back to Kin, why couldn't she save him? Why was she sent back to the past if she couldn't save him? Maybe it was all a bad dream and she would wake up soon. Kayla came to a gate that looked familiar; it was the gate to Kin's property.

"This is it, girl," she told the spotted horse. "I see the barn."

Kayla dismounted and let the horse drink from the water barrel . Steel was there. Kayla's heart skipped a beat, Kin and Steel were always together, could he have made it out alive, she hoped. But as she looked around she saw nothing, no one, just a pile of ashes where a home had once stood, where she had spent one of the most wonderful nights of her life. She flashed back to seeing Kin in the tub, water glistening off his muscular body.

"Who are you?" came a voice from behind, bringing her back to the present.

Kayla turned to see a small older man staring at her. His wire-rimmed glasses slid down to rest on the end of his nose.

"My name is Kayla Price." Maybe she shouldn't have told him that but he looked harmless.

"Doc Price," he said, holding out his hand to her.

Kin had mentioned him. She shook his hand.

"I'm the closest thing Kin has to family, where have you been, girl?"

"The Reeds..."

"Yep, that's what I figured, how did you get away?"

She opened her mouth but before she could speak he interrupted.

"Never mind, all that matters is you did. Come with me, I want to show you something."

Kayla followed the old man. He led her to the rock. She dropped to her knees at the sight of it, she'd seen this rock many times, she'd chosen it as a centerpiece for her flower garden, but yet looking at it now had a whole other meaning. She now knew the man who's name was scratched into its surface, she couldn't help but cry for him.

"I should have been able to save him."

Doc put a reassuring hand on her shoulder. "Come on, missy, it's time to get going."

"Where?" she asked.

"Home."

"I don't even know where home is," she said honestly.

"For now it will be at my home."

They got on their horses and rode away from the Parsons Ranch.

"So how did you get away from the Reeds?" he asked again.

"I shot Teddy."

"Lordy, girl, did you kill him?"

"No, I just shot him in the foot."

"How did you get away from the other two?"

"They were passed out from too much liquor and once Teddy was alone it was easy."

"When they wake up they will be looking for you, and the first place they will look is here. We'd better move along faster."

Steel was much bigger and stronger than her little spotted horse. She only seemed to be holding them back.

"We need to let that mare go," Doc told her. It wasn't easy but Kayla climbed onto Steel with Doc and they made better time, but riding the large animal made her dizzy.

It was dark by the time they reached Doc's cabin. Her backside hurt so much it was all she could do to slide off the animal's back. They took the horse to the barn and then Doc ushered her into the cabin. He led Kayla to a small room in the back of the cabin. The door opened slowly and there she saw Kin spread out across a bed on his belly, an excited squeal escaped her, she quickly put her hands over her mouth.

"I… He…"

"Yes, he is alive."

"Then why did you let me believe that he was dead?"

"I wasn't sure if I could trust you."

"I understand." After all, he didn't know her, but even so it hurt her feelings to know that someone didn't trust her.

"He made me promise to find you, and get you back safe."

"And you did."

"Actually, you found me."

"It doesn't matter who found who, it just matters that we are all here, safe."

"Amen, little lady."

Doc crossed the room and felt Kin's forhead, he felt a little clammy but the fever had broken. Doc pulled the sheet down and checked the wound. Kayla flinched at the sight of the bullet hole. She still couldn't believe that he had survived it.

"The bullet missed all the important stuff, he will be back to normal in a few weeks," he told her. "He might sleep for a few days straight," he warned.

"That will be all right, he needs to rest and heal... I'd like to sit with him if you don't mind."

"I'll make you a deal, young one, if you clean up and eat yourself something I'll let you watch over him for me."

"You have deal." They shook on it and the Kayla took the most relaxing bath she had ever taken. She really needed to wash the stink of the Reeds from her.

She was so exhausted and yet she was terrified to fall asleep—what if she disappeared? She did want to go home... But now that she knew Kin was alive she didn't want to leave him again.

"Come on, girl, he'll wake up when he is ready." Doc steered her out of the room and into another. "This is where you will sleep."

"But where will you sleep?"

"I have a cot in the kitchen."

"I can't let you do that, you sleep in here and I'll use the cot."

"No, no," he insisted. "You will sleep here like I said."

She was much too tired to argue so she did as he said. She must have fallen asleep the minute her head hit the pillow.

The sun peeked in the window of her little bedroom. She heard Doc's voice, she didn't think much about it until she heard Kin's voice as well. He sounded weak but he was talking. She jumped out of bed, tripping on the long nightshirt that she had borrowed from Doc. She landed on the wood floor with a thump but before Doc could reach her she had jumped up again and was in the doorway of Kin's room.

Kin was sitting up in the bed, she could tell that he was still in a lot of pain but he was awake. Their eyes met.

"I thought you'd died," she told him.

"It takes more than a Reed to kill me," he said. He shifted and winced in pain.

"Take it easy, boy, you ain't healed yet." He handed Kayla a tray with a glass of milk and what looked like a bowl of applesauce. "I gotta take care of the animals, you can take care of the patient, make sure he eats every bite of this." And then he walked out.

There was an awkward silence in the room.

"I should have listened to you, Kayla."

"About what?"

"About your dream, I should have listened to your warning."

"You didn't know, I have to admit, I even think I sounded crazy."

"The Reeds… Did they…hurt you?"

"No, they didn't ."

"Did they…"

"They didn't do that either… They implied that's what they intended but they didn't get the chance."

Kin couldn't stand the thought of another man touching her, he was so deeply in love with this woman already that it wasn't funny. After Kelly had broken his heart he swore he would never love again but he couldn't help himself. He stared at her, he thought she was absolutely beautiful.

"You know, Doc carved your name in a rock, it looks like a grave marker, he let me believe you were burried under there for a while."

"Yeah, he can be mean like that sometimes."

Kayla picked up the spoon and dipped it into the sauce.

"I can feed myself," he told her, taking the spoon from her, groaning as he tried to lift it to his mouth.

"Apparently you can't." She took the spoon and put it to his mouth. He reluctantly submitted, and let her feed him like a child.

SEVEN

Present time

Shelly slammed her fist down on the table, she was furious.

"I don't care what you say, Jake, Kayla is alive, I refuse to believe that she could be dead."

"She's been missing for two weeks, no one has seen or heard from her, I don't want to think the worst either, but I know that she wouldn't just leave without telling one of us."

"It doesn't mean that she's dead." She shook her head back and forth. She would never believe that her best friend was dead.

"I know, Shelly, I didn't mean to upset you, maybe she just needed to get away for a while."

"She wouldn't just go, she was taken away," Shelly insisted.

"Who would take her?" Jake asked, he was just as worried as Shelly was, but in all honesty he had to admit that Shelly was starting to get on his last nerve.

"The same man that was outside her bedroom window, the same man that was on the hill, the night before she disappeared…whoever that man is."

"So what do you suggest we do, Shelly?"

"We just wait longer, maybe the man will call back with a ransom demand."

"I think you have been watching too many movies."

"You can think whatever you want to, Jake, but I'm telling you Kayla is being held somewhere against her will, and it's obvious the police don't believe me but you could; we are all friends and you know as well as I that Kayla would never leave without telling one of us, and if she could call us she would."

Jake put his head in his hands, she was right and that's exactly why he thought she was…dead.

"And don't you even think it, Jake. If she were dead I would know it, I'd feel it."

"All right, Shelly, I guess all we can do is wait… But in the meantime I have to keep this ranch running, if… I mean when she gets home she will kill me if this place isn't in top running order."

"You're right, and she will be back, Jake, she will."

Jake pulled shelly into his arms and hugged her tightly. They were in this together, Kayla was a best friend to both of them and they had to be strong for her sake.

Shelly had been camped out on Kayla's couch every night since she went missing, it was if she had vanished into thin air. The newest ranch hand, Matt, actually said that she had; he claimed that he was the last person to see her, the police questioned him but they let him go when they could find no evidence that he personally had anything to do with her disappearance. And people just didn't vanish into thin air, it just didn't happen.

1876

Kayla woke up in Doc's bedroom, where she had been sleeping for the past few nights. Doc had left to help a woman give birth, he wasn't expected to return for a few days. Kayla had been bathing and feeding Kin while he recovered from his gunshot wound. She was falling hard for the man, but it was always in her mind that she didn't belong in this time, and someday she would go home, she didn't know when or how, but she knew that it would happen and she would be alone again.

She drifted back to sleep but only for a moment. She felt Kin's warm breath on her neck. At first she thought she was dreaming but when she opened her eyes, there he was, his face freshly shaven, wearing a silly grin.

"Are you always so cheerful in the morning?"

"Only when I know there is a beautiful woman in the next room."

"Really?"

"Yep."

Kayla sat up quickly, it had suddenly dawned on her that Kin was up and walking, by himself. "You're walking."

"I've been doing that since about the age of one or so." His sensce of humor still intact, he did a little dance to show her that he was fine. "A little stiff but I think I'll live."

"I'm so glad you're better." She hugged his neck and pecked him on the cheek.

"I knew you would be, this means I can feed and bathe myself again, you don't have to do that for me anymore, you're no longer my slave."

"I'm free," she shouted, doing a jig of her own.

"Oh, I see how it is, and all this time I thought you actually enjoyed giving me all those sponge baths."

"I did… Maybe I should give you just one more." Her smile faded, as did his.

"I want to make love to you, Kayla Price." He drew closer but she pulled away. He wanted her and Lord help her she wanted him too. He followed her and turned her toward him, he kissed her, she kissed him back, the very taste of him sent her head spinning. She knew that if he wanted to take her she would not be able to stop it from happening, she didn't want it to stop.

Kin gently pushed the nightgown off of her shoulders. It fell to the floor, leaving her exposed. She lay back on the bed, he stared at her for the longest time before he spoke. "You are so beautiful," he managed to choke out.

"Thank you."

"Help me undress," he asked, pulling her hands to his pants.

"I can't." She pulled her hands back, suddenly feeling shy.

"Yes, you can." He pulled her hands back, this time to his his shirt. She unbuttoned the buttons one by one. He stared into her eyes the entire time.

Once she had removed his shirt she ran her hands over his smooth bare chest, he was a strong man. She hesitated again when her fingers went to his pants, he took her hands in his and together they removed his pants. Kayla was breathless as he stood before her nude and fully aroused, her mouth grew dry and suddenly it was very warm in the room.

"It's hot in here, don't you think?" she asked him, fanning herself with her hand.

"It's about to get a lot hotter."

He lay down on the bed beside her, she wanted to touch him but she held back. He kissed her deeply, a kiss that sent electric pulses running through her. She had never felt that kind of friction with anyone before. Of course she had only made love to one other man—the man she thought she would marry—but thankfully he had just dumped her and married another woman.

"What are you thinking about, Kayla?"

"Just how good you make me feel."

"It gets better," he promised.

He poised himself over her, kissing her lightly on the neck, then taking his lips to her breasts, lingering for a moment, then down to her navel and back to her neck, he entered her gently, she moved with him and moaned in pleasure, it was the best she had ever felt, and she couldn't hold back any longer. She writhed in pure ecstasy…then she wept.

"What's wrong?"

"Nothing."

"A lady doesn't just cry for no reason, did I hurt you?"

"No… It just felt so good."

"I'm glad, but is that any reason to cry?"

"I'm crying because I'm already in love with you and I know that we can't be together." She covered her face to hide her tears.

"Why can't we?" He pulled her hands away from her face.

"I have to go home, I have friends that I'm sure are worried about me."

"But now you have me, we can make a home together." He stroked her brow.

"It isn't that easy, Kin, I have a life, I have a ranch."

"So do I, Kayla, but I want you to make a new life with me."

"I couldn't possible stay here."

"Why not? So far you have done real well. You might as well get used to being here, you don't even know where your home is or how to get back to it."

"I have a feeling that as soon as I let myself believe I'll be here forever I'll be pulled back to my own time and lose you."

"I'm sorry, sweetheart, but I still have a hard time believing that you're from the future."

"I know it's hard to believe, but I am, Kin. I am."

"So why did you end up here, with me?"

"I think I was sent here to save your life from the Reeds."

"Maybe that's part of it, I just think we are meant to be together."

"If that were the case we would have been born in the same era—not about a hundred years apart, don't you think?"

"I don't know what to think, Kayla." Kin stood up and paced the floor, running his fingers through his hair.

"All I know is that one day I wake up to what I think will be a day just like any other, only it's not: I find a woman passed out and bleeding outside my front door, and as crazy as all her talk is about being from the future and men walking on the moon I end up falling in love with her, only for her to tell me that she does not want to be with me."

"I never said I didn't want to be with you, I just don't know if it's possible to stay with you, I can't believe after what just happened that you think I wouldn't want to be with you."

"Do you love me, Kayla?" He took her face in his hands.

"I do love you, I do."

"I love you, I know we have only known each other for a few short days but I know that I want to be with you for the rest of my life. I want to make love to you every day, I want to father your children, so why won't you stay with me?"

"Let's just live in the here and now, not think about tomorrow, make love to me again, Kin," she pleaded.

He did as she asked. This time it was slower and longer, they skyrocketed together. Kayla collapsed on his chest, weak and out of breath.

"After that, you'd be crazy to think I won't do anything in my power to keep you with me," he told her.

"After that, I want to be with you forever, Kin Parsons." She looked into his eyes and could see the love he felt for her, but she also caught a glimmer of doubt.

"I don't know about you, but I'm famished."

"I could eat something," she admitted.

They walked into the kitchen naked and unashamed.

"I hope Doc doesn't come home," Kayla said.

"He sees naked people all the time."

"Yes, but not roaming around in his own home."

"That's true."

Kin fried up some bacon and eggs and put a plate in front of her.

"It's nice to have a man cook for me."

"I've been cooking for myself for a long time, no reason that should stop just because I fell in love."

"Good."

"I believe you were supposed to say something like 'I would love to cook and clean for you and be your love slave, making your every wish come true.'"

"Really?"

"Well, it would be nice to hear but I don't expect it."

"Well, how about we take a nice warm bath right now and discuss this further?"

"I think that's a great idea."

"I'll race you to the tub." He ran through the cabin ahead of her.

"Didn't your mother ever tell you not to run in the house?"

"Yes, but I didn't listen."

They both hopped into the large tub, water spilling out onto the floor.

The door to Doc's cabin opened and closed with a slam, Doc ran in, his hair was disheveled and his clothes looked as if he had worn them for days straight.

"Is something wrong, Doc?" Kin took Kayla in his arms, trying to hide her nakedness from Doc, but the old man didn't seem to notice.

"Them Reed boys is after Kayla."

"But they don't know where she is, she is safe here."

"Not for long. After birthin' that babe I headed for the saloon as usual. I heard them talkin, they are planning to search every cabin until they find her."

Kayla shifted in the tub. "Did they say when they might start looking?"

"They already are, they just took a break to get drunk."

"Get dressed, Kayla, we have to leave now."

"Where are we going to go?"

"I don't know yet, but they will come here, they know Doc and I are close and they will look here sooner than later. Doc's right about that."

"This is ridiculous, we shouldn't have to run."

"No, we shouldn't, but if we don't they will find us and kill us for sure."

Kayla knew very well what they would do to them. She dried herself off and dressed.

Doc had finally calmed down and looked at Kin. He could tell there was something different about him.

"I assume you're feeling better."

"Yes, I feel fine, Doc."

"Love does wonders for a man."

"Is it that obvious?"

"It is, don't think I didn't notice that you weren't alone in that tub when I came in."

"Doc, while you were gone I made up a will," he said, changing the subject.

"Why'd you do that for?"

"Because I'm supposed to be dead. And the only way that I can keep them Reeds from taking my land is if I had a will made up saying that if I die you get my land and everything on it."

"Are you loco, son?"

"No, I'm perfectly sane…for a dead man. You take this to the law and promise me that you won't let them take my land from you."

"I can't promise, but I will do everything an old man can do to keep it from happening. Where are you going?"

"I don't know, but we have to leave."

"You take good care of that girl, I don't know why but I feel a special bond with her."

"I'll take very good care of her, Doc, I promise you that."

Kayla put on the only clothing that she had; it wouldn't do much good if it were to get cold, she might freeze to death. She looked out the window of the bedroom, no sign of the Reeds— yet.

"I'm sure these will fit you."

Kayla jumped at the sound of Doc's voice behind her.

"What are these?"

"These dresses belonged to my wife, I just couldn't bear to get rid of them when she passed, I always knew that someone would be able to use them one day."

"You are the sweetest man, Doc, I'm going to miss you."

"You'll get over it." He blushed.

"I'll never get over you, Doc, I'll remember you forever." She saw tears in his eyes.

"You'd better get changed, the Reeds will be expecting to see you in those clothes, what there is of them." He turned away, wiping the moisture from his eyes.

"Will you tell Kin I'll be right there?"

"Will do, little lady."

Kin sat patiently waiting, as patiently as he could that is.

"What in tarnation is taking so long?"

"Now, son, you know how women are."

"Yes, Doc, I know how most women are but Kayla is certainly different from any I've met so far."

"Different can be good." Doc sat down in his rocker and lit up his old pipe.

"Maybe, Doc. Maybe."

Kayla strolled into the room and twirled around in her new dress. It was a nice fit but she was not used to wearing anything like it. It was floor length and her dresses were much shorter and tighter fitting; of course she had to keep reminding herself that things were much different than they were in her time.

"I sure hope you can ride in that dress."

"I can do anything I set my mind to, Kin Parsons."

"I hope so, we have to move fast to keep ahead of them Reeds."

"I'm ready when you are, boss," she said, giving him a salute.

"Thanks for digging that bullet out of my back, Doc."

"It was nothing."

"Oh, it was something, Doc," Kayla interrupted. "If it weren't for you I would have lost him…and I just found him." She gave Doc a hug and a quick kiss on the cheek before jumping on the back of a little mare that Doc had given her to ride.

"She's a keeper, son, don't let this one get away."

"Oh, I don't plan on letting her go."

Kin and Kayla rode off side by side, neither of them really

sure of where they were going, but knowing that they would be together was reassuring.

They rode in silence for what seemed like hours but had only been minutes.

"Do you know where we are going?" Kayla asked.

"I want to stop by my place before we move on…forever."

"Do you think that's wise? I mean, the Reeds could already be there."

"I doubt that they have finished their drinking yet."

"But when they do that's the first place they will look for me."

"I don't expect you to understand, Kayla, but I need to see my place, just one more time. I promise I won't let them hurt you. They caught me off guard once but it won't happen again."

"I understand," she told him, and she did. If she had known she would not see her home again she would have enjoyed it more; she would have told her friends how much she loved them if she'd known she would not see them again. *Shelly must be beside herself,* she thought.

When they reached Kin's place Kayla could feel the tension radiating off of Kin's body, he looked at the remains of his cabin, it was ashes now. He scanned the hillside for a moment. Something caught his eyes. He headed Steel up the hill and Kayla trailed behind.

"Where are you going?"

"Up the hill."

"I can see that, but what for?"

"I don't know yet."

Kayla said no more, she just followed his lead. When Kin reached his destination he jumped off of Steel and squatted down behind a large tree.

"What in the world are you doing?"

"Shhhh, get down."

Kayla did as she was told. She squatted down beside him and followed where he was looking. She saw a tall, thin, lightheaded woman staring down at something. She looked sad. She may have been crying, it was hard to tell from that distance.

"Who is she?"

"That's Kelly."

"Kelly Hall?" The woman he had been engaged to.

"Yes."

"She looks pretty." *What?* That was all she could come up with?

"She's very pretty." Kin looked at her sadly.

"You're still in love with her, aren't you?"

"In love...no."

"Then why do you look so sad?"

"I feel sorry for her, she is very unhappy."

"How do you know that?"

"Kelly used to be full of life, happy all the time... Now she always looks like that."

"Are you sure you don't love her anymore?" It was silly for her to be jealous but she just couldn't stand the thought of what Kin and Kelly had once shared.

"She's leaving, let's go."

"You're avoiding my question."

"We don't have time for silly talk, I want to see what she found so interesting."

Kin gasped when they reached the spot where Kelly had stood. There was the rock, the one that was to be his grave marker. He knew that Doc had done it, he'd told him he'd done it, but the shock of seeing it for himself was a lot to handle. People were supposed to think he was dead. He didn't have any family but he had some friends who might actually miss him, Kelly being one.

"I guess that settles it, I'm dead to the world."

"But you're not really dead, isn't that what counts?" She put her arm in his and they stared at the ground where the rock lay. Kayla had that weird tingly feeling again.

"I hear horses, we have to move now," he told her.

Kayla stood still.

"Get on that mare and move, woman," he demanded.

Instead Kayla bent down and tried to move the rock from its place—it wouldn't budge.

"In a minute, help me move this, will you?"

"We don't have a minute. They are getting closer."

"Please," she pleaded with him.

"You're a crazy woman." Kin rushed to her side and helped her roll the rock over. The ground looked odd, it had a green tint and it didn't look solid, it looked as if… As if one could fall right through it.

"What the hell…"

"I think this is our way out."

"What are you talking about?"

"Look at the ground, it isn't normal. It isn't natural. This is our way out of here, maybe a way back to my home, to my time."

"I'll tell you one thing that isn't normal, that's you, we have to get out of here now."

Kayla looked up, the Reeds were in sight now, if she could see them then they could see her and Kin as well.

"Get on your horse, damn it, maybe we can still outride them."

No, there was no way they could outride them now, their best hope was to take that chance and hope that she was right.

She grabbed Kin's hand and pulled him to the ground. "It's our only chance, we have to jump in."

"We blew our chance to get away," Kin mumbled.

The Reeds were only feet in front of them now.

"I'll be dog gone, Pete, he ain't dead after all."

"I'll kill him this time fer sure." Pete took his gun out of its holster and took aim at Kin.

"This time I'll shoot him in the heart."

Kin looked at Kayla. He took her hand in his and smiled at her. "I don't know how or if this is going to work but it's the only shot we have now."

Kayla started the count of three.

"What are you two doin'?" Pete asked suspiciously.

"We are leaving," Kayla said matter-of-factly.

"You gotta get past us first."

"Two...three..." They jumped into the green abyss and the wind began to whirl around them. Dust was so thick no one could see what was happening, it only lasted for a few seconds. When it was over the Reed men stood in dismay. Kin and Kayla were nowhere to be seen.

"Where did they go?"

"They just disappeared."

"That can't be," said Pete.

"Them horses are still here, they can't get too far if they're on foot."

"Then get to lookin'," Pete demanded. He walked to where Kin and Kayla had been standing, the ground looked normal again.

"Witchcraft," he told himself. He knew there was something different and weird about that damn woman and now he had the answer: she had to be a witch and she cast a spell to get them out of there. What else could it have been?

EIGHT

Kin and Kayla plunged into the future and found themselves smack in the middle of what appeared to be some kind of riot.

"What happened?" Kin looked around. When he didn't see the Reeds it was obvious to him that Kayla had been right about the ground being their escape.

"We did it, we got away," Kayla chimed.

"Yes, now how do we escape this?" Two men were fist-fighting in front of them. One man punched the other so hard that the man almost plowed over Kayla.

"I don't know yet."

"But this is your world, isn't it?"

"No. I'm not sure exactly where we are or what year it is but this isn't where I came from."

They watched as dozens of people broke out storefront windows and carried out food and all types of items.

"They're looting."

"What?"

"They are stealing."

"Why?"

"Because they have no food or money."

"None of them? Why not?"

Kayla looked to her left. She saw police officers coming

toward them. She grabbed Kin's wrist and pulled him along behind her. "We have to get out of here?"

"Why?"

"Because these people are going to be arrested and we don't need to be in the middle of it."

"We haven't done anything wrong."

"They don't know that. If we are in the middle of thieves we will be mistaken for thieves as well, guilt by association I think it's called."

"Where are we going to go?"

"I don't know, just walk," she snapped at him.

"I'm beginning to think I should have taken my chances with the Reeds."

She ignored his remark. Walking along the street, Kayla noticed there were no horses.

"Look at these roads, they are no good for the horses' hooves."

"Well, have you seen any horses?" she asked him.

"No. Why is that?"

"They have other ways of getting around now."

"Like what?" he wanted to know but his mind was not purely on transportation at that moment; he was watching a woman and her children sleeping on benches and the ground.

"Why do you suppose they are sleeping outside?"

"Apparently they have nowhere else to go." Kayla answered his questions the best she could while keeping her pace.

"Where are the men? Why are they not taking care of their families?"

"Maybe they can't."

"Why can't they? I'd have to be dead to not take care of my own wife and children."

Kayla stepped into the middle of the road. "I think we landed in the middle of the depression."

"What the hell does that mean?"

"It's a long story, it happened before I was born, I just know what I've read about it."

"What did you read about it?"

"Things went terribly wrong for a lot of people, some lost everything they had, others lost their lives, some people committed suicide just to escape."

"Only a damn fool would kill themselves, especially when they have families to worry about... I don't like this place, let's get out of here."

"Now you understand how I felt when I found myself lost in a different world."

"I understand a little better now," he admitted.

A little girl ran up to Kin, her face was dirty and her hair needed a good brushing, her clothes were tattered and torn. She asked him for some money, he looked in his pockets but they were empty. He bent down to the little girl.

"I'm sorry, sweetheart, but I don't have any money." The little girl began to cry.

"I'm sorry, sir, I've told my children not to beg, but we haven't eaten in two days," a thin, middle-aged woman said, taking the girl by her hand.

"It's all right, ma'am."

"How long have you been living on the streets?" Kayla asked.

"Two months now, my husband was a jumper."

"I'm so sorry."

"Don't be sorry for us, miss, we will manage." She took her child's hand and walked away.

"What did she mean her husband was a jumper?"

"He jumped out of a window, or off a roof, whatever the case may be, he committed suicide and left his family to fend for themselves."

"He deserved to die," he said matter-of-factly.

"Kin."

"I'm sorry but he wasn't much of a man to leave his family alone to suffer, he should be right alongside them."

"But that's still a cruel thing to say."

"And leaving your wife and children with nothing isn't cruel? He had a choice, Kayla, he made the wrong one, and I don't feel sorry for him, not at all."

"Okay, you have a right to your opinion."

"But you don't share it?"

"I don't want to argue with you, we have to figure out how we are going to eat and where we are going to sleep."

"I hadn't thought about that... I'm no thief, Kayla," he said, knowing they would have to steal to eat.

"I'm not either, but we have to do what we have to do."

They walked in silence until they came upon a little grocery store, there were people all around.

"It should be easy to get something from here, matter-of-fact, eat what you can inside, less chance of us getting arrested once we leave the store."

Kin scanned the shelves of the store, there was very little left to choose from. He picked up some apples and stuck them in his pocket. Luckily he had on a jacket or he wouldn't have been able to hide anything. Kayla found some cheese and crackers, she shoved some in her mouth, she saw chocolate bars and couldn't resist, she managed to smuggle six of them.

They didn't say a word to each other until they were a safe distance from the store, they found themselves back at the same park where they had seen the little girl.

"Why did we come back here?" he asked.

"I think we both know why we came back here," she said, pulling the candy bars from her dress, she looked up just in time to see the little girl run to Kin and jump into his arms, he barely had time to catch her.

"Well, you look happy," he told her.

"I like you," she said.

"I like you too... I have something for you." He set her down and pulled an apple from his pocket.

"I thought we agreed not to smuggle anything out of the store."

"We did, but I don't think you paid for those chocolate bars, did you?"

"You got me."

"I'm sorry, sir, I told her not to bother you."

They looked up to see the girl's mother again.

"Sara, where did you get that apple?"

"I gave it to her," Kin replied.

"That's very nice of you, sir, but we can't accept—"

"Please let her have it," he interrupted . "I can only offer you these apples for your family but I would like for you to have them."

"I have four chocolate bars as well, it would make us very happy if you would accept them, even if it's not a very well-balanced meal," Kayla added.

"It's better than no meal at all, thank you, both of you." The woman wept.

"You're welcome," they said in unison.

They watched as the mother and daughter walked back to the bench, where two young boys waited for them to return.

"I feel better now, how about you?" she asked.

"I'd feel better if we were somewhere else, this depression is getting depressing."

"Did you happen to save any of that fruit for us?"

"As a matter of fact I did." He pulled two more apples from his pocket. And she pulled two chocolate bars from her dress and held them up.

"You are perfect, woman." He kissed her full on the lips before sitting on the bench.

"Not quite, but close enough." Kayla sat down beside him and snuggled close. It was chilly and for everyone's sake she hoped it wouldn't get any colder during the night.

They ate and then lay down on their backs, it was a clear, starry night. They fell asleep in each other's arms.

When morning came Kayla found herself alone. She sat up and wiped the sleep from her eyes. "I know I'm not dreaming this, Kin was with me last night," she said aloud. Panic set in.

"You weren't dreaming, fancy face, I'm here."

She whirled around to see Kin behind her with a devilish grin on his face.

"What are you up to?"

"I've been walking, looking for a way to get us out of here."

"Have you found one?"

"No, not yet."

"I can help you look."

"Well, four eyes are better than two." He giggled.

"Better make that three because my eyes really aren't that great anyway."

"I'll take what I can get." He took her hand in his and they began to walk along the empty street. They soon came along the same little store where they had stolen from the night before. Kin's stomach growled.

"Either you're hungry or there's a wild animal after us." She looked behind them nervously.

"I can't help it, I'm a growing boy."

"The only thing growing on you is your gut." She patted his belly.

"That's not entirely true, just looking at your pretty face is making another part of me grow."

Kayla's mouth dropped open. "How on earth can you think about that at a time like this?"

"Sorry, I just look at all these people, and I can't help but think at least I have you."

"Yes, you do have me." She looked into his eyes and saw the genuine love.

"What do you say we go in there and get us some food?"

"I don't know, I don't have a good feeling about this one."

"We have to eat, don't we?" He kissed her on the forehead and entered the store before she could stop him. He walked from shelf to shelf, grabbing the smallest things he could find and stuffing them into his pockets.

Kayla waited outside. She saw a policeman walking toward her. Her palms began to sweat, she tried not to look guilty.

"Morning, ma'am."

"Morning," she replied. She prayed that he wouldn't go inside the store, he kept walking.

"Can I help you find something?" the store clerk asked Kin.

"I was looking for some crackers… My wife is with child and it's all she can keep down these days."

"I'm all out of crackers."

"Okay, well, thank you." He walked quickly out of the store and grabbed Kayla's hand.

She whispered that there was a cop close by and they walked the opposite way.

"Stop, thief." The store owner was outside looking and pointing directly at Kin.

"I suppose you're the thief he's talking about?"

"Yep."

"What do we do now?"

"I suggest we run." And that's what they did, they ran and soon four police officers were in foot pursuit. He searched frantically for a way to escape them and suddenly a miracle before his eyes… Two horses.

"I don't guess I have to tell you what my plan is?"

"I call the small horse."

They untied the horses and jumped on, they made the horses run as fast as they could, until they could no longer see town.

"I think it's safe to slow down now," he told her after a few minutes.

"Oh my gosh, did you see how fast I was riding?" she asked proudly.

"I did, honey, you're getting the hang of this horseback riding."

"I know, I almost like it," she admitted.

"I can see a house up the road, maybe we can get some water for the horses."

"This looks familiar," she said as they got closer to the home.

"Everything looks familiar to you," he told her.

As they drew closer to the house Kayla began to get excited. Her heart raced and she started to laugh.

"What's so funny?"

"That house, it looks a lot like mine."

"I thought that you said we were not in your time."

"We aren't, this road would probably be paved in my time. I'm sure we are still in 1932."

"How did you find out what year we are in?"

"While you were stealing breakfast I was reading a newspaper and it had the date on it… By the way, did you make it out of there with any food?"

Kin pulled a stick of beef jerky and a chocolate bar from his shirt pocket and passed them over to her. "Nothing but the best for my lady, unfortunately that's all I could grab."

Kayla's mind was no longer on the food. "I really think this is my house."

"I see a pond, maybe the horses can get a drink there," he said.

"Shouldn't we ask permission first?"

"It doesn't look like anyone is home."

"No, it doesn't, but they could still be asleep."

They went ahead and led the horses to the pond and let them drink.

"Look at that tree, Kin." She pointed and his gaze followed.

"What about it?"

"Look at it, come on." She led him to the tree.

"Hey, it's the tree that I carved my and Kelly's initials in."

"Yes."

"But how can that be? You said this looked like your house."

"It is, it was built in 1923."

"But that would mean it's built on my property."

"I know."

"So how would your family have gotten my land?"

"You are so slow, Kin." She thumped him upside the head.

"I don't appreciate that remark." He rubbed his head.

"I'm sorry, I didn't mean it."

"I guess Doc must have sold the land."

"No, no, he said he would keep it."

"He had to have sold it at some point."

"No, remember when we first met and you asked if I was related to Doc because we have the same last name?"

"Well, now that you mention it I remember that."

"Obviously it is no coincidence that we share a last name."

"This is so strange." He paced back and forth. "Has the world gone mad?"

Kayla ignored him. "What is Doc's first name?"

"I think it was Alvin, I've just always called him Doc."

"Alvin... That was my great-great-grandfather's name."

"Are you telling me Doc was your great-great-gramps? That might explain why he felt partial to you."

"He said that?"

"Yep, said he felt a bond with you."

"That's sweet. He promised he wouldn't let the Reeds get your land, and he didn't."

"He always kept his promises."

"We keep being led here, Kin, that must mean that eventually we will get home soon."

"To your home," he told her.

"To our home, Kin." She hoped that once they reached the year 2007 they could stay and be together forever.

"We should find my gravestone, it's obvious that's the only way we can travel to a different year."

"We'd better find it fast because the cops have found us."

"Way out here?"

"Stop, stop!" Police were yelling and running towards them with pistols drawn.

"Didn't we just go though this?" he asked.

"Déjà vu!"

"What?" he asked.

"I'll explain what it means later, just run."

And so they ran, finally they came across the rock, just as they expected there was the familiar green glow in the ground.

"Help me roll this thing, Kay."

"I thought you could do it by yourself, you big strong man."

"Give me a break, I'm still recovering from a gunshot wound."

"I have to do everything," she huffed.

"This is no time to joke, honey, they have real guns, and believe me it hurts like hell to get shot."

"I believe you." They pushed on the rock until it moved over and displayed more of the green ground.

"Ladies first." He extended his hand in front of him.

"I think we should hold hands again, I wouldn't want to be separated."

"Good idea, sweetheart." He hadn't thought about that before but it could happen and Lord help him if he ended up in the future without Kayla—he would really be lost.

They closed their eyes and held on tightly to each other's hands just like they had before.

"Did you see that?" one cop asked the other.

"I didn't see anything." He rubbed his eyes.

"They just disappeared, you're telling me that you didn't see them dissapear?"

"I didn't and neither did you."

"But I did see it," he argued with his partner.

"If you go back to the station house and tell this story they will think you are crazy and you'll never live it down, is that what you want?"

"No."

"Then it stays between us, we both saw it but we can't tell anyone."

The younger cop rubbed his jaw for a minute, thinking.

"Yeah, you're right, I didn't see anything. They were just too fast for us and got away."

"That's right, they had too big of a lead."

2007

Shelly knelt down on her knees in one of Kayla's flowerbeds, she pulled weeds left and right.

"What are you doing, Shelly?" Jake stood behind her.

"I can't just leave these weeds here, if Kayla was home she would have already had this done."

"You shouldn't worry about it."

"Kayla would just die if she came home and her flowers were choked out by all the weeds."

Jake knelt down and put his arm around her. "I don't think Kayla is coming home, honey."

Shelly paused. "Please don't say that, don't talk like that."

"The last thing I want to do is upset you, Shelly, but I just don't think she is coming home."

"I'm starting to think you might know more than you're telling us," Shelly accused.

"I promise, I know nothing more than you do."

Shelly wanted to believe him, she didn't want to think that Jake could be involved in her disappearance, but there were things that didn't add up, and she was just going to come out and tell him.

"I was going through Kayla's desk and I found a key, it belongs to a safe."

"So?" Was this supposed to mean something to him?

"I opened it… I found her will, Jake. She left everything to you."

Jake was dumbfounded, why would she do that? After all, Shelly was her best friend.

"I don't understand why would she do that, Shelly. You're her best friend."

"She did will me her car, and a great deal of money, but the house and the land she willed to you."

"I had no idea."

"But didn't you?"

"Are you implying that I killed Kayla because I knew she had left me her house and land?" Jake was heartbroken that she would actually think he could have done something so horrible.

"I didn't say that."

"You've known me since the first day I came to work here, how could you think that of me, Shelly?"

Shelly looked directly into Jake's eyes, she noticed the dark circles under them, lack of sleep and worry. A guilty man, a truly guilty man would not have that look about him.

"I'm sorry, Jake, I'm just looking for answers. I know you had nothing to do with her disappearance." She tried to convince herself of that.

"It's all right, I guess if I were you I might think the same thing."

"You are going to keep working the ranch for a while, aren't you?"

"I'll stay on, at least until my own home is ready."

"What do you mean?"

"I've been building my own home, I have some land just on the west side of Kayla's."

"Since when?"

"When Kayla's dad hired me I told him up front that I wanted my own cattle ranch, he knew my working here would be limited. He encouraged me to work for my dreams. I would have been on my own ranch already had he not passed on. When he did I promised myself and him that I would stay and look after Kayla until she was okay on her own, until I had found a trustworthy replacement to run this ranch. I've been paying on the land for the last six years and I've been building on the house for the past six months."

"Does Kayla know about this?"

"I haven't had the heart to tell her about it yet." She knew the answer to that before he told her, of course she didn't know. She would have told her if she had, and she wouldn't have left her land to him in her will.

"She didn't know."

"So when do you plan on leaving here?"

"As soon as Kayla and I find someone else to run the ranch. If she doesn't come back—"

"Say no more, if she doesn't come back you'll sell it, right?"

"Listen, Shelly, I didn't ask to be put in her will, I don't want the land, I have my own."

"You should have told her your plans, if she'd known she might have done something different. I know she would be heartbroken to see her house and property be sold off to a stranger."

"Why did she leave it to me in the first place?"

"Why? Because you love this place and you have worked your ass off to keep it running smoothly and she thought that if she died and left it to you, you would keep it forever and continue to do so, it would be like keeping it in the family, Jake, because that is what she thinks of you as...family."

Jake bent his head, feeling as if he had done something wrong by having his own place and wanting to have a life of his own other than the Price Ranch. He walked out the door without saying another word to Shelly.

Matt met him on the way out.

"What is it, Matt?"

"I wanted to talk to you about the ranch."

"Is there a problem?"

"Do you think that Miss Kayla is ever coming back?"

"I don't know, she could be dead for all I know."

"What if she is dead, Jake? Who would be in charge of the ranch?"

"I don't know that, Matt." Matt hadn't been the first hand to ask what would happen to their future, all the employees were in limbo until Kayla was found.

"I think you do know, I bet she left you in charge of it all if she was to leave."

"And why would you think that?"

"Come on, Jake, you run the place, this place ain't nothing without you."

"What are you getting at, Matt?" Jake's patience was wearing thin with this kid.

"I want to buy this place."

"I can't sell it, it does not belong to me."

"I bet it will soon enough, if I'm thinkin' right."

"Kayla will be coming home soon enough and then you can ask her if she wants to sell out, I know she won't but it's up to you if you want to ask."

Jake led his horse away towards the pond, he passed the place where he had last seen Kayla, by that big rock that he had promised to move for her. He felt a chill run through him, stopping him in his tracks.

"What the hell was that?" he asked himself. He stood for a moment until the feeling had passed and then continued on.

NINE

June 1957

Kayla and Kin woke up to find themselves in an old junkyard, there were crushed cars all around them.

"Where are we now?" he asked her, as if she would automatically know where they had ended up.

"It looks like a scrap yard."

"What are all these contraptions?"

"Cars, remember? I told you about these."

"They look funny, what's wrong with them?"

"Well, they are old, they are all junk now, waiting to be crushed. At one time they were nice and and fun to ride in, not like the bumpy horse buggies from your time."

"I'm just an old-fashioned guy, I happen to miss my bumpy old buggy and I really miss Steel."

"I know, honey, I know you miss your horse, I shouldn't have said anything about it."

Kin looked around, they were sitting inside of something.

"What are we sitting in, by the way?"

"Oh my gosh." She began to get excited when she realized what they were sitting in.

"It's a 1957 Chevy." She jumped out of the car and circled it, it was cherry red and brand new.

"This looks like a brand-new car. I wonder why it's in the junkyard?"

"Who knows." Kin was checking out the strange vehicle.

"I wonder if we are actually in 1957."

"How do you work one of these things?" Kin was back inside the car, behind the steering wheel.

"I would show you if there were any keys in it, I bet it belongs to the owner of the wrecking yard."

"I like this contraption, it's shiny."

"I always wanted one of these cars." She scooted closer to Kin and spotted the keys dangling from the ignition. "The keys are in it."

"So what does that mean?" he asked.

"Switch me places and I'll take you for a ride."

"That would be stealing again."

"I know, but this is my dream car, I always wanted to drive one of these."

"And I thought you only dreamed about me." He put out his bottom lip and pouted like a child. "I guess you're tired of me already."

Kayla put her arms around him. "I could never be tired of you… Now trade me places."

She crawled over him until she was positioned in front of the steering wheel.

"We can't take this car, we shouldn't even be sitting in it."

"You're such a worry wart, let's just take it for a quick spin and then bring it back. Please, please," she begged.

"I know we shouldn't but you're not going to stop until you get your way, are you?"

"Nope." She turned the key until the engine turned over. "Sit back, I'm going to take you for a ride that you will never forget." She stepped on the gas and the car began to inch forward. Kin held on to the dash.

"Having fun yet?"

"I'm not sure what to think yet."

Kayla drove around the scrap yard looking for a way out. She saw a gate but it was closed.

"Can you get out and open the gate for me?" she asked.

"Sure." He did as she asked, he pushed open the gates and when he turned back to get in the car he found himself looking into the eyes of two vicious dogs, and they looked hungry.

"Get in the car," she ordered.

"I'm afraid to move."

"Why?"

He pointed. Kayla looked and saw the mean dogs as well.

"Oh boy, walk very slowly to the car." He did as she said, the dogs didn't move until he picked up the pace. By the time he reached the car they were biting at his heels.

"Jump in the window, hurry."

Kin dove into the open window and Kayla stepped on the gas and got the heck out of there. Kin was upside down for what seemed a long time.

"Slow down, will you, I'm getting motion sickness."

They were about a half mile down the road before the dogs stopped chasing them and she slowed down enough for him to sit upright in the seat. Kayla was still laughing.

"What do you find so funny?"

"You should have seen yourself, hanging out the window with a couple of mutts biting at your heels."

"Yeah, it probably did look funny…to you."

"I'm sorry."

"You shouldn't be, I like to see you laugh."

"Okay, hold on tight, here comes the fun part." Kayla stepped on the gas, the tires squalled and smoke rolled, they were doing sixty in no time.

"Slow down, you're going too fast," he told her.

"This isn't fast." She stepped harder on the pedal until they were doing ninety. "This is fast."

"I think I'm going to be sick," he told her. "You'd better stop."

"Are you serious?"

"Very serious, stop the car," he ordered.

Kayla pulled over to the side of the road and watched Kin open the car door and all but fall out, she heard the most awful sounds coming from him, it almost made her sick listening to him.

"Are you all right, honey?"

"I'll live." He crawled back into the the car and kept his head down.

"I'll find somewhere to park and we'll walk from there."

"We should take this back where we found it."

"Do you really want to see those dogs again?"

"No, but it would be the right thing to do."

"I know, but the right thing these days isn't always the right thing for us."

"True," he agreed.

Kayla drove slowly until she came across a park. There was no one around, it was a nice sunny day, she wondered why the park would be empty on such a nice day. She pulled over and turned the engine off,she leaned over and put her head in Kin's lap.

"Do you feel any better?" she asked, as he stroked her forehead.

"I'll be fine, just a little embarrassed."

"Don't be, we all get sick sometimes. Is there any way I can make it up to you?" She put her head up and winked at him.

"I might take you up on that offer a little later, right now I'd like to walk for a bit."

"Okay, but stay where I can see you."

Kin got out of the car and walked to a cluster of trees. He thought he could truthfully say he'd just had the worst experience of his life—he hadn't been that scared when he got shot.

Kayla rummaged through the car. She found some money, and when she opened the trunk of the car she found two blankets and some clothing. It looked like some one had been packed for a trip and she had stolen their car right from under them. She knew she should feel guilty for doing it but she didn't. She always wanted to drive a 1957 Chevy and now she had. She only wished that Kin had enjoyed it as much as she had. She sifted through the clothes and found some that looked like Kin might fit into them; at least he could wear the shirt. She giggled when she pulled a poodle skirt out of the bag. She'd always wanted to wear one of those—now she would have her chance. It was past time to get out of the long dress that Doc had given her; after all, she had been wearing it since 1876, people would notice her in that and she didn't want to be noticed.

Kayla crawled back inside the car and when she emerged she was wearing the poodle skirt with a white blouse and scarf. She sort of felt like a teenager again. She scooped up the blankets and the clothes she had taken for Kin and headed for the cluster of trees where she had seen him walk to earlier.

"Kin where are you?"

"I'm over here, honey."

Kayla found him sitting against a tree with his head between his hands. He looked disturbed still.

"Are you still sick?"

"No, I'm just a bit overwhelmed, things are happening so fast, it all feels like a dream and I just want to wake up, but if it's all a dream that would mean you are too."

"I'm not a dream, sweetheart; as hard as it is to believe, everything we have been through is very real, but I know how you feel."

"Do you? I've been ripped away from my home, my world and put here where things run a hundred miles a minute and I'm not just talking about that contraption you call a car but everything is faster, I don't think I can keep up with it, Kayla. I'm a simple man meant to live a simple life in a simple time."

Kayla didn't know what to say; sure, she could remind him that she too was ripped from her home and her lifestyle but what good would that do? It wouldn't make either of them feel any better, so instead she sat beside him. He put his head in her lap and she stroked his light brown, hair trying to give him some sense of comfort. Before long he was asleep.

TEN

Kayla carefully lifted Kin's head and laid it down on a blanket. She covered him up with the other one. she counted the money that she had taken from the car: twenty dollars. It wasn't much but then again twenty dollars in 1957 went further than it did in 2007; they could eat for a few days on that. First thing she had to do was get as far away from that car as possible; by now the police would know it was stolen and probably be looking for it. Kin was snoring loudly; she figured he'd be out for a while so she got back into the car and drove it down the road until she found some tall weeds, that's where she parked it. They would really have to be searching to see it there. Then she walked on into town and found a burger place. She ordered three cheeseburgers, two fries and two chocolate shakes to go.

"That's a lot of food for one lady," the boy behind the counter said to her.

"It's not all for me."

"Oh…is there a man with you?" The boy looked around.

Kayla wondered why he was asking. Should she be worried about her safety? Was he going to follow her? Maybe the word had already gotten out about the car thieves and they already knew she was one of them.

"No, I'm just picking this up for a friend."

"Oh, well, you have a nice day."

"You too." Kayla hurried back down the road. She hoped the food would still be warm and the drinks cold when she got back to Kin; she hoped he hadn't woke up and thought she'd left him. When she got back Kin was right where she had left him and just starting to wake up.

"Did you go somewhere?"

"I've been gone for hours and you didn't even miss me."

"I was so tired, I'm sorry."

"Don't be sorry, I just hope you're hungry."

"I'm famished, where did you get the food?"

"I found some money in the car."

"So you took it? And where is the car?"

"I parked the car behind some tall bushes and then I walked into town and got the food."

"And where did you get the clothes and these blankets?"

"All of it in the car, I guess we ruined someone's plan for a trip."

"Is this what people are wearing nowadays?"

"Yep. I don't think these pants will fit but this shirt should fit you just fine."

"Yeah, yeah, let's worry about the clothing later. Right now I just want to eat." He scooped up a burger and took a bite, then he took a sip of the shake. "This drink is wonderful."

"I thought you might like it."

"You know what I like."

"Do you think it's safe for us to go back into town?"

"Why? Is there a reason to go back?" he asked.

"Well, I saw an ice cream parlor and I just wanted to take you there, my dad used to take me for ice cream all the time."

"Whatever you want, honey, you lead and I will follow."

"Great, let's go."

"Now?"

"No time like the present." She grabbed his hand and pulled him up, dragging him from the safety of the trees.

"Can we find our way back?"

"I'm sure we can." Kin let out a moan. He was not sure about going back into town. It always seemed to end with someone or something chasing them.

It was dusk now. The town was already lit up and people were milling about, there seemed to be an abundance of teenagers, he noticed.

Soon they found themselves in front of the ice cream parlor that Kayla had spoken of.

"Let's go in."

Kin held the door open for her and he followed her in. There were a few kids sitting around a table and there was a couple dancing in the middle of the floor. The music was loud and strange, nothing he'd ever heard before.

"What kind of dancing is that?"

"It's called the twist, come on, let's try it."

"No thanks, wouldn't want to hurt myself."

"Okay, suit yourself." Kayla got out on the dance floor and started dancing with the kids. He watched her closely, the way her body turned and twisted with the music. Before long she had a partner; a young boy was in front of her grinning ear to ear, he knew he was only a teen but it still bothered him that he had the nerve to approach his woman. Kayla glanced over at him and saw that he was less than pleased so she thanked her dance partner and returned to the table.

"You didn't have to stop on my account."

"I didn't, that dancing takes a lot out of you, I'm tired."

"Well, you're not as young as they are."

Oh no, he didn't just say that.

"You're not a spring chicken yourself, mister," she snapped.

"I didn't mean to upset you, I was merely stating that they are still very young...and you..." He could tell that the more he talked the deeper the hole he dug.

"I'm going to get our ice cream. I'll be back."

"Good idea."

When Kayla returned to the table she had a bowl with one scoop of vanilla, one scoop of chocolate and one scoop of strawberry and two spoons.

"Well, you should like one of these flavors."

He took a spoon and dug in, trying each flavor.

"I like them all but the pink one is my favorite."

"That's strawberry."

"It's delicious."

Kayla leaned across the table and kissed him.

"What was that for?"

"Just because...I love you."

"Maybe we should get back to our spot in the park," he suggested.

"That's a good idea, it seems to be getting warm in here." Kayla stood. "Are you coming?"

"Just one more second, honey, I seem to be a bit excited, might be a bit embarrassing to get up now."

Kayla's face blushed. "I didn't realize I had that much of an effect on you."

"Well, you do, honey."

"I need to use the ladies' room anyway, I'll be right back."

As Kayla washed her hands at the sink she looked at her reflection in the mirror. She was blushing and smiling, she felt good, the best she had felt in a long time. Kin was the reason, she was in love, he made her feel like this, he made her life worth living, she wanted to get home but only if it meant having Kin with her; if she had to she would spend the rest of her life running from year to year as long as it meant they could be together.

Kin stood at the front door waiting, he seemed to be very interested in something happening across the street.

"What's going on out there?" she asked.

"I think the law is looking for someone, that is the law, isn't it?"

Kayla looked outside. She saw four officers talking to a young couple. She decided the best thing for them to do was leave before anyone saw them.

They stepped out the door holding hands and headed back for the park.

Their exit from the ice cream parlor didn't go unnoticed. The young woman whispered something in her husband's ear. He in turn whispered in the officer's ear. Kayla knew immediately that they were on to them. Kin hadn't seemed to notice that the same red car they had taken a joyride in earlier was now parked alongside the curb and she had no doubt that the couple were the owners and that they probably recognized their own clothing that Kin and Kayla now wore. She fully expected them to chase them but they didn't.

They walked along the street until they returned to the park where they had left the blankets; where they planned to spend the night .

"It's good to be home," he said.

"What? This isn't home."

"It is for tonight, and as long as I'm with you anywhere we are is home, as long as we are together."

Kayla pulled him into her arms and took a deep breath, he smelled wonderful. "I need you tonight," she whispered to him.

He took her face in his hands and kissed her with such passion it made her dizzy.

"Make love to me, Kin."

"I thought you'd never ask." Kayla stretched out on he blanket and Kin hovered over her, kissing every inch of her body, leaving her skin on fire. Then suddenly he stopped.

"What is it?"

"I hear something."

"It's just my heart pounding."

"No, baby, I hear voices."

Kayla sat up. "I don't hear anything."

"I do, we have to leave." He stood, lifting Kayla with him. Against her wishes they left the safety of the trees; now she could hear the voices that Kin spoke of, they were getting closer. They stopped hehind a big oak tree.

"Look, Carl, these are our blankets," they heard a woman say. They had just missed being caught in a very awkward situation.

"This must be their hideout. They might be coming back."

"We should get more help and surround the park, if they are here they won't be able to leave, and if they come back someone will be able to get them. The good thing is we already know what they look like, now we just need to find them."

Kin looked at Kayla, knowing that they were on the run once again. Would it never end, he wondered.

"Walk slowly or they'll hear you," he warned her.

"It's a good thing I'm in such great shape with all the running we've had to do," she joked.

He looked her up and down. "I can't argue with that. You do have a great shape."

"Why is it that evey time we attempt to make love someone starts to chase us?"

"I don't know, but I'm half tempted to just take you right here and whoever sees us sees us."

"Kin, that wouldn't be such a good idea."

"I know it. But dog gone, Kayla Price, I love you so much I can't stand it, I want to make love to you every day and I want to right this minute."

"I love you too, Kin, we will have our time, just not right now."

"Well, what do we do now?"

"I suggest we look for our rock and get out of here before we get caught."

"Why is it that rock is never here when we need it?"

"Stop right there, you two," said a high-pitched male voice from behind them.

They turned and found themselves staring into a flashlight.

"Where did you come from?" Kayla asked.

"I should be asking you that question," said the voice, "I know the cops are looking for you two, the news is all over town."

"So you're not a cop?" Kin asked.

"Are you kidding? I can't stand those cops,but I do want to know why they are after you, what have you done?"

"We haven't done anything," she lied.

"Those bastards chased me once for nothing too." He spat on the ground.

"I'm sorry to hear that, we really should get going."

"I'll give you a ride if you want one, you won't get far on foot."

"I don't know…" Kin started.

"That's very nice of you to offer but Kin gets carsick."

"I won't drive fast or nothing."

Just as they were about to turn down the man's offer again they saw flashing lights headed their way.

"I guess we need that ride after all," she said.

"Yee haw! Get in, kids."

Kin and Kayla slid into the backseat of the car and before they had the door shut the man sped off, squaling tires. Kin groaned. "I knew this was a mistake."

"What other choice did we have?"

"Where do you want me to take you?" the man asked.

"Turn left and keep going until I tell you to stop," Kayla directed.

There were three police cars on their tail.Kayla held on to Kin, he seemed to be turning paler. She tried to watch for her turn but it was so dark she was afraid that she might miss it. Meanwhile the man in the driver's seat was having the time of his life.

"I think I'm going to be sick," Kin warned.

"Oh, man, you look like you're turning green."

"Watch the road," Kayla yelled to him.

He turned his eyes back to the road and swerved just in time to miss a car. Kin rolled the window down, sticking his head out and vomiting.

"Feel bettter?" she asked.

"Not really."

"I ain't never seen anyone turn green before."

"Turn here," Kayla ordered.

"Which way?"

"Left."

The man cut the wheel to the left, they could feel the tires coming off the ground and soon the car was skidding to a stop on its side.

"I never want to ride in one of these things again." Kin groaned.

"That was great, let's do it again," the man said.

"I don't think so. We have to get moving before they catch up to us."

"Oh come on, I know where we can get another car."

"I think we should just walk from here."

"Where you walking to? Can I come with you?"

"I don't think that's a good idea," Kayla told him.

"Why not?"

"Because the police are after us and we don't want to get you in trouble."

"But you said you didn't do anything."

"I lied."

"What did you do?"

"I killed a man," she said with a straight face.

"What?"

"You heard me."

"I don't believe you killed a man." He looked over at Kin for confirmation. He nodded yes, still holding his stomach.

"Why? Why did you kill a man?"

"Because he wouldn't shut up, he just kept talking and talking and asking question after question…kind of like you're doing right now." She gave him a crazy look.

The man looked scared now. He let out a little whimper before running off into the dark.

"You didn't have to scare the poor man."

"I think I did, he wasn't going to leave."

"Okay, it serves him right for turning the car over and almost killing us."

"Yeah, he's the crazy one, not me."

"If you say so. Now what do we do? Where do we go from here?"

"You see those lights in the distance?" she asked him.

"Yes."

"If I'm correct, those are the lights to home, our rock is almost in sight now."

Kin took a step forward but the carsickness hit him again and he doubled over to vomit at Kayla's feet.

"You're so romantic," she told him.

"Sorry."

"Don't worry about it, we have to get moving…if you can."

"I can." He hoped he could, she must think of him as a big sissy, a man who got motion sickness, he never got sick while riding his horse; he didn't understand why riding in a car would make him sick. They held hands and headed for the hill. Kin felt something dripping on his hand. It wasn't raining, he finally noticed that it was blood—Kayla's arm had a large gash in it.

"You're hurt." He tried to stop but she insisted on moving.

"It's nothing."

"It is something, you're bleeding badly."

They neared the house. A porch light came on and a young man stepped outside on the porch, stopping Kayla in her tracks.

"What's wrong?"

"That man…"

"What about him?"

136

"He's my dad."

"He looks so young."

"He is young, I guess he would be about eighteen."

"Still a boy."

"I have to see him." She started to run for the porch but Kin grabbed her arm.

"It's not a good idea."

"Why not?"

"Do you really have to ask that? What are you going to say to him, you're his daughter? He'll call the police."

"You don't understand, I have to see him one more time."

"But he won't be the same person you remember, it's not a good idea."

But Kayla was already running away from him and towards the man who would one day be her father but now was only a stranger. By the time they reached the porch the boy had a shotgun aimed in their direction.

"Who are you?" he wanted to know.

Kayla could tell that he was more frightened that she was, even though he held the gun.

"We... I..."

"Spit it out, lady, before I shoot you for trespassing."

"We didn't mean to bother you, sir." She looked into his eyes, silently begging him to recognize her. He dropped the gun. And they took off running for the hill, for the rock.

The boy made no attempt to chase them.

"What happened back there, Kayla?"

"I don't really know, but I got to see my dad again, even if he didn't know who I was."

When they reached the top of the hill they could hear voices.

"It sounds like our crazy man has led the police right to us."

"Yeah, we'd better find that rock fast."

"I see the green glow already," he told her.

"Stop, you didn't think you could outrun us, did you?" yelled a group of angry men.

"We aren't running," she told them.

"Yeah, I didn't think you would be that stupid.Put your hands on your head," he told them.

"Sorry, man, we have to go," Kin added.

"You two aren't going anywhere."

"Oh, I think we are," he told them.

They held hands and once again leapt into the green glow. They knew that they were going through time but they couldn't have gone far because the ride was a quick one.

July 1966

They dropped from the sky into a body of water. Kayla let out a scream of pain, her hurt arm had been slammed against the water, it felt like smashing into a block of concrete.

"Are you all right, Kayla?" She was now lying face down in the water. She wasn't moving. He pulled her head out of the water and swam to the bank, he shook her a bit and finally she coughed up some murky water and rolled to her side so that she could breathe easier.

"I thought you had gone and died on me," he told her.

"You're not getting away that easily." She sat up and stripped off a piece of her skirt to wrap around her arm.

"You need a doctor."

"I'll be fine," she insisted.

"I wonder where we landed this time."

"Look, there's people over there." She pointed.

"Looks like two women."

Kayla took a closer look. "Those aren't women," she told him. "At least one isn't."

"No man is going to have hair to his waist."

"He looks like a hippy."

"A what?"

"In the sixties and seventies a lot of men wore their hair long and they were called hippies."

"So how do we find out what year it is?"

"We ask."

"I don't want to talk to those people; they scare me from back here," he admitted.

"Come on, honey, Kayla will protect you," she teased.

"Oh, for Pete's sake."

Kayla frowned at him. "Wrong choice of words."

He didn't mean to bring up the name Pete; after all, he was one of the reasons they were in this situation.

They walked from the lake until they reached the couple.

"Hey, what's up?" she asked.

"Not much... Just smoking some Mary Jane... Want some?" the man offered.

"No thanks," she told him.

"Who's Mary Jane?" Kin whispered to her.

"I'll tell you later, whatever you do don't smoke any of it."

"Could you tell me what year it is?" she asked.

The man laughed at her and looked at her poodle skirt. "Where you been, lady? Stuck in the fifties?"

"You could say that, yes."

"Well, it's time to ditch the poodle skirt and get with the rest of us in 1966."

"Thank you, and I would like to ditch the poodle skirt; however, I don't have any other clothes to change into, we are kind of on the run," she confided.

"Well, you stick out like a sore thumb in those outfits, it won't take long for whoever's looking to find you."

"Do you have any clothes we could borrow?"

"As a matter of fact I do... What's your name?"

"Oh, I'm Kayla and this is Kin." She pulled him up beside her.

"Nice. I'm Moon and my old lady over there is Sky."

"What kind of names are—"

"Those are lovely names," Kayla interrupted. All she needed was Kin to start something with this guy.

Sky took her by the hand. "You men talk and we will be right back."

The women climbed into a Volkswagen van and shut the door behind them. Sky pulled out a purple dress and some white sandals for Kayla to wear and she handed her a string of beads to put around her neck.

"So are you and Kin married?"

"No, but we hope to be some day."

"So he's pretty hip?"

"Yeah, I guess you could say he's hip. Are you and Moon married?"

"No, we believe in free love. You should love as many people as possible and never be held down to just one person."

"Really?"

"Yes, would you like to stay here for the peace rally tonight?" she offered.

"Peace rally?"

"We expect at least one hundred people, maybe a few more."

"What are you going to do?"

"We are going to demonstrate how to make love not war."

Kayla's eyes got big, this could not be a good thing. "I'll ask Kin."

"I would love to get my hands on your Kin… I mean, that would be groovy."

When Kayla stepped from the van she saw that Kin had changed his clothes as well, he had on a loose-fitting pair of pants and a shirt that was so bright she understood why he was also wearing sunglasses.

Sky reached Kin before she did, she rubbed her hand on his chest. "You look groovy," she told him.

"Is that good or bad?"

"You're so funny."

"Kin, I'd like to take a walk." Kayla didn't wait for an answer, she just pulled him by the arm and dragged him behind her.

"What's wrong?"

"That woman was all over you."

"What do you mean?"

"She wanted to get you in her bed."

"She was just being polite."

"It was more than that, believe me."

"My dear Kayla, I do believe you're jealous."

"Don't forget to ask him about the rally," Sky yelled to them.

They walked back toward the water that she had almost drowned in earlier.

"What's a rally?"

"The kind she's talking about is more like an orgy."

"What's that?"

"You don't want to know."

"Yes, I do."

"It's when a group of people get together and make love."

"Oh… Oh, you don't mean…"

"Yes, they swap lovers."

"Oh, we can't stay for that." His face was red.

"Thank you."

"I'm not sharing you with anyone."

"I feel the same way about sharing you, it's not going to happen."

"I guess we need to tell them thanks but no thanks and get back on the road."

As they rounded a cluster of bushes they landed straight in the middle of a circle of people, groping each other, some were already making love and others were still looking for a partner. Before she could even blink Moon had come up from behind and grabbed her hand, pulling her away from Kin, and Sky was already all over Kin. Moon kissed her full on the lips, she pulled away and slapped him, he smelled of beer and marijuana , it made her sick. She saw Kin running to her, he was furious.

"What's with your chick, man?" Moon asked him.

"She doesn't want you to touch her, and neither do I."

"Man, that's what were all here for. To make love not war."

"That's not why we are here, thanks for the clothes but we are leaving now."

"What's your problem, man?"

"I was taught that we make love with the one woman we are in love with, not any one that's willing to. You have no respect for women or yourself for that matter."

"Dude, you just don't know what you're missing. Take Sky, she will show you and I'll show your woman." He reached for Kayla again. Kin grabbed his hand and bent it back. She heard it snap and Moon cried out in pain.

"I warned you not to touch her again."

"Just leave, man, just leave," Moon begged.

Before long other hippies had come over and started to throw punches at Kin, Sky slapped Kayla and she slapped back, it was a full-fledged bar fight except they weren't in a bar. So much for the making love not war rally. Kayla tightened her fist and was ready to swing when someone grabbed her from behind. She swung at him and then she quickly realized it was a cop she'd just clocked.

"I'm sorry, I thought you were one of them," she told him.

"Aren't you one of them?" he asked.

"Oh no, we just wanted to leave and they wouldn't let us so Kin hit Moon and then it's all kind of a big blur."

"If you're not one of them then what are you doing here?"

"We kind of got lost and ended up here, our clothes got wet and they loaned us some dry ones, we were just trying to leave when Moon grabbed me and said he wanted to make love and when I said no he tried to force me and Kin came over and I think he broke Moon's hand and then the others jumped him and—"

The cop held his hand up. "Okay, lady, stop talking for a minute."

"Okay." She tried to catch her breath.

"I'm taking you all to jail," the officer announced.

"Oh but—"

"Tell it to the judge, lady," he cut her off.

"I will, just as soon as we get there."

"It will be morning before you see him."

"You mean we have to stay all night in jail?"

"Yes."

"What about bail?"

"So you're familiar with jail, are you?" he asked Kayla.

"Well, no. But I get to make a phone call, don't I?"

"Sure."

That was great, she could make a phone call, but whom would she call? It looked like they would be stuck in jail for the night.

"I can't go to jail, I just can't," she pleaded.

"Come on, lady, or I'll drag you."

She did as he told her, she hoped her good behavior would get her free, otherwise she could be there for a long time. She had never been in jail, she had no idea how it worked, she only knew that she could possibly get out on bail, if she had someone to bail her out.

She had been in the holding cell for three hours now, she was being held with ten other women, including Sky. She hadn't seen Kin since they'd been hauled in.

Kin sat in a holding cell with several other men. Moon had two black eyes, a busted lip and a broken hand for what he had done , or tried to do to Kayla.

"You didn't have to bust my face up, man," Moon told Kin.

"I told you not to touch Kayla."

"I didn't think you were serious."

"Now you know how serious I am when it comes to the woman I love."

"Yeah, dude."

"Kin Parsons, you're free to go," said the officer at the door.

Kin looked up at him, surprised. The door opened and he stepped out.

"What about the rest of us, man?" Moon asked.

"You losers are here for the night."

Kin stepped out into the hallway, where he saw Kayla waiting for him, she hugged him tight. "How did you get us out of here?" he asked her.

"I used my feminine wiles."

"What?"

"I talked to the judge, I simply told him that we were in the wrong place at the wrong time, I told him the truth, and he let us go."

"Just like that?"

"Sort of… He knows my father."

"I know you didn't tell him we were traveling through time and that actually you won't even be born for three more years."

"I told him everything."

"No, you didn't."

"He asked about my family and I told him that my father is my uncle and that I was on my way to his home to surprise him with you, my fiancé, when all this happened, I told him we only acted in self-defense against the hippies."

"And he believed you."

"Of course, it's the truth… Most of it is anyway."

"Well, we'd better get as far away as we can before he sees your dad, or your uncle, and finds out the truth… You have me confused now."

"Sorry. I guess we'd better get on the road."

"Which way from here?"

"West, out of town seven miles."

"I don't understand why we keep ending up so close to your home every time."

"I don't either, I just hope the next time it puts us in the same year I left, I wonder how long it's been since I left? I wonder if they all think I'm dead?"

"It does no good to wonder, sweetheart, let's just keep trying until we get there."

ELEVEN

Kayla and Kin left the courthouse and headed west once again.

"I gotta tell you, Kayla, I'm tired, I need some sleep."

"What? You didn't sleep in the jail?"

"Yeah, with one eye open, can't rest much that way."

"I suppose not."

"If we ever get back to your time, maybe we can sleep and make love without having to worry about someone chasing us."

"I want to make love to you more than I want to sleep," she told him.

"I wouldn't be able to make love to you properly without some rest first."

"What? You want to sleep before making love?"

"I'm an older, wore-out man, sweetheart."

"Maybe I should find someone younger," she teased.

"Oh no, let me rest for thirty minutes and you'll be the one who can't keep up."

"Really?" She loved to joke with him, sometimes he took her serious, but he was starting to understand her and know her better; the more he was with her the more he loved her.

"You know, for all the trouble we've had I'd almost rather go home and face the Reeds."

"Don't say that."

"I miss my home, I miss my boring everyday life on the ranch."

"I miss my life too. But I wouldn't trade the time we've spent together for anything."

"I wouldn't either, but I can't help but think that we are not meant to be together."

"How can you say that, Kin? After all we have been through I think we are meant to be together; after all, I was sent to save you from being killed."

"Maybe my life was only spared to help you get back to your life, maybe once you get home I will be hurled back to my own time and die anyway."

"Stop it! Don't talk like that. You aren't going to die."

Kin took her by the shoulders and shook her. "How do you know that? You can't know what's going to happen."

"No, I don't, all I know is that I want to marry you and have a baby with you and…and—"

"You want to have a baby with me?" he asked.

Kayla looked at the ground, she hadn't meant to say all that, it was true but she hadn't planned on telling him that so soon.

"No."

"Then why did you say it?"

"I do want a child with you, I just didn't mean to tell you about it."

"Make up your mind. Kelly told me she loved me and wated to have a child with me and then she up and married someone else a few months later. I don't want to go through that again."

"I would never do that to you, Kin, I love you and I want to have a child with you."

"What if I told you I wanted to go home and live, back in my time?"

"I guess I would have to say yes."

"You would?" He was shocked.

"I would miss my friends and my home but if it were the only way I could be with you then I would go."

146

"I just don't know if I could live like this." He spread his arms wide. "You're the only reason I'm not searching desperately for a way to get home, I should be trying to move backward, not forward."

Kayla was crying, she continued to walk straight ahead without looking at Kin. She could now see her house, it was a different color from the last time they were here, it was now a pale blue, she didn't like it very much but blue was her mother's favorite color and her parents would now own the house she would grow up in .

"It looks like we made it again," he said.

"Yep! It looks that way." She kept walking.

"That man on the porch must be your father again."

"It looks like him," she said, but she never looked that way, she was sure it was her father but she just didn't have the guts to look at him, she didn't want to cry again and right now it was all she could do to keep from bawling like a big ol' baby.

"Maybe we can get to the other side of the house without him seeing us."

"Who is that with him?"

"Probably Mom," she said, not looking towards the house.

"No, it's a child."

"I don't know who it would be."

"Is it you?"

"No, I won't be born for three more years, maybe it's a cousin or a friend's child."

As they drew closer to the house Kayla could hear her father's voice, he was talking to the child. She stopped and turned to look at them, the child looked like he could be two or three years. She watched her father set him down and he ran to the screen calling for his mommy. Kayla's mom appeared in the doorway; she opened the screen and lifted the boy into her arms.

"What's Momma's big boy up to?" she asked him.

"I didn't know you had a brother," he told her.

"I didn't know it either." She walked faster toward the house.

She had to see this kid, she had to know if she really had a brother and if she did, what had happened to him? Why didn't she grow up with him? Why did she never get to know him?

"I don't think it's a good idea to let them see us," he warned.

"Please, I have to know what happened."

"Okay, but let's not stay long."

"Thank you."

The little family of three had seen them approaching and stood up to greet them. "Hello, it's a nice day, isn't it?" The lady introduced herself and her family.

"I'm three today," said the little boy she called Tyler.

Kayla went to her knees and looked the little boy in the face, he had the same green eyes that she had, he looked as if he could have been her own child.

"Is today your birthday?" she asked, holding back the tears.

"Yes, I'm three," he repeated.

"I have a present for you, if that's okay with your parents." She looked to them for approval and when they didn't object she reached for her neck and removed a pendant. She handed it to the boy. It was a heart pendant. He took it from her and gave her a silly grin.

"It's a girl's," he giggled.

"You don't have to wear it but maybe someday you will know a girl you want to give it to."

"Thank you," he told her, giving her a hug.

"You're very welcome." She got back to her feet and faced her parents again, they had simply told them their names, never explaining why they were walking on their property or where they were headed.

"Would you like to stay for supper?" her mother asked.

"Are you sure that wouldn't be any trouble?" She looked to Kin, he nodded okay so she accepted the invitation. She followed her mother in the house to help with supper while Kin stayed on the porch with the boys.

While in the kitchen peeling potatoes Kayla couldn't help but to ask a few questions.

"Is Tyler your only child, Mrs. Price?"

"Please call me Tina," she insisted.

If she only knew how odd it was for Kayla to be standing beside her mother calling her by her first name, even stranger her mother would be younger than she was.

"Tyler is our only child, we would like to have another someday."

"He's adorable.I bet you love him to death."

When Tina didn't answer Kayla stopped peeling potatoes to look at her. Her mother sank down into a chair and started to cry.

"Did I say something wrong?"

"No, no… Tyler, he's, he's very sick, the doctor said that he wouldn't live to be three, but today he turned three, it's a big day for us."

Kayla sank down beside her mother and held her hand. "I'm so sorry, I had no idea."

"How would you? You just met us."

"What's wrong with him?"

"He has a rare type of cancer."

"Can't they do something for him?"

"No, there is nothing…"

The men entered the kitchen and when Mr Price saw his wife crying he didn't need to ask, he often found her alone crying, trying to prepare herself for what was to come any day, to prepare herself for the loss of her child.

"What are you crying about?" Kin asked Kayla.

"Oh, nothing, I just smashed my finger and it hurt," she told him as Tyler entered the room.

"Then why is Mommy crying too?" he asked.

"You know I don't like to see someone in pain, just like when you get hurt and cry, Mommy cries with you too."

"Does your mommy do that too?" he asked Kayla.

She looked to her mother. "Yes, Tyler, my mommy does that too.

"Does he know?" she whispered to her mother.

"Yes, he knows, but he is stronger than we are about it."

"What are you two women whispering about?" Kin asked. He didn't like being out of the loop, he wanted to know what was going on.

"I'll tell you later." Kayla gave his hand a reassuring squeeze.

The five of them sat sown at the dinner table and Kayla ate the best meal that she had since her mother had passed away.

"That was so good, Mrs. Price."

"Thank you, Kin, like I told Kayla, you can call me Tina." She began to clear the table.

"I think we will sit in the parlor and have some coffee," her dad said.

"Yes, dear, I'll bring it to you in a moment."

The men sat talking and watching Tyler play with his new birthday toys; his favorite seemed to be the bright red fire engine.

"Are you sure that we haven't met before?" Stan Price asked Kayla as she handed him his coffee.

"I don't think so."

"You look so familiar."

"I think I would have remembered you if we'd met. We thank you so much for your hospitality, but we should be going now."

"We have plenty of room, if you need a place to stay for the night," he offered.

"That's very generous but we really should go now."

"I'll walk you out," he offered.

"We can find our way, thank you!"

Kayla hugged her mother good-bye, something she didn't get to do before she died.

"Tyler, I hope you had a wonderful birthday, thanks for letting us share it with you."

"Thank you for the necklace." He held it up with pride.

"You're welcome."

The little boy hugged her neck. She held him tight, not wanting to let him go. She didn't want him to go, she wanted to save him, save him for her parents, save him so that she could grow up with him. But she couldn't do that, she let him go and he walked back into the house, the screen door slamming behind him. They stepped off the porch and headed to the same familiar rock where they always seemed to find themselves when it was time to make the next journey.

"Here we are again," he told her.

"Yes, here we are."

"Are you ready to go?"

"No." She looked back at the house. Her family was inside. She wanted to be there with them. "My brother is sick, he's dying."

"I'm so sorry." Kin's heart hurt for her.

"They never even told me about him, why wouldn't they tell me I had a brother?"

"Maybe they couldn't."

"They have pictures all over the house of Tyler but I never saw one, it's like he never existed. Why wouldn't they want to see his face and remember him. Why wouldn't they tell me how special my brother was?"

"Kayla, honey, don't do this to yourself, it's obvious they love that little boy so much and maybe it was easier for them to not look at pictures and not talk about him. People deal with loss in different ways."

"Maybe you're right."

Kin rolled the rock over. "It's now or never."

Kayla found herself praying to God that this time they would land in her own time, she needed her friends, she needed to be in a familiar place, she loved Kin and she wanted to be with him always but right now she felt so lost and now she realized that was how Kin was feeling earlier that evening.

151

They held hands and spiraled into time once again, landing on a stack of hay.

"That was better than landing in the lake," he told her.

"Yes, it was." They looked around, it looked like a barn.

"Maybe we are in your barn, maybe we made it to your time," he told her.

"Maybe." She stood up and walked to the door, peeking out. "It's dark outside."

"Are you serious? Maybe we can get some sleep before someone starts to chase us."

Kayla returned to his side, she could see the light from the full moon spilling in through the cracks in the walls.

"Are you sleepy?" she asked.

"Aren't you?"

"Tired, not sleepy."

"How can you not be sleepy? We couldn't have slept more than four hours in the past three days."

"Theres something else we haven't been able to do for the past three days." She reached for her zipper and let the dress she had borrowed from Sky fall to the floor.

"I want to resist you, lady, but who am I kidding." He reached for her, pulling her down to the hay pile with him. He kissed her with such force.

"Ouch."

"Sorry, I want you so much right now I can't stand it."

"Then take me, make love to me," she begged.

Kin left her just long enough to shed his own clothes, he was fully aroused and couldn't hold back any longer, he entered her quickly. She stifled her cry, she didn't like it so rough but she wasn't about to tell him to stop, she needed him now more than ever, she needed to feel his love. They rocked until finally they found release together, she swallowed her tears so that he would not know she had been crying the whole time they were making love, not that he was hurting her but just everything they had been through, all the things that she had found out about her own life that she should have already known, it was all taking its toll on her. She swallowed hard.

"I'm sorry, Kayla, I'm so sorry." He stroked her hair... She fell fast asleep.

He watched her sleep for a while before falling asleep himself. Kayla dreamed, she saw a little girl playing in a field by herself, it was her when she was young, the girl looked up into the sky and on a puffy white cloud she saw the same curly-haired little boy who she now knew had been her brother. He sat looking down on her, a smile on his face, telling her that he was okay and she should not be sad for him. She cried in her sleep.

Kin watched as she slowly woke up and took in her surroundings. "Was it a bad dream?"

"No, actually my brother told me not to worry about him and that he was fine, he's in a better place and now he, Momma and Daddy are all together again." She stood up and walked around, finding herself sore from the rough lovemaking.

"What's wrong, did you hurt yourself when we landed?"

"I don't think so."

"Then why are you walking like that?"

"I think it has something to do with our lovemaking." She blushed.

"I'm sorry, I shouldn't have been so anxious."

"Don't apologize, I loved every minute of it." She pulled her dress back on. "The sun is up, dare we go outside in the open?"

"I don't think we can hide in here forever."

"You first." She dared. him.

Kin opened the door a crack and peered out. He saw the same familiar land that had kept drawing them back over and over again.

"It looks like we're home again."

"Do you see anyone?"

"No, just some cattle grazing."

"Please, let it be," she prayed, putting on her sandals, she opened the door and took a deep breath.

A wave of hot air slapped her in the face.

"It feels like summer." She fanned herself briefly. She looked around. "There's a pool in the backyard!" she yelled.

"A pool?"

"Look." She pointed.

"It's a pond."

"Kind of, only it's kept clean, the animals don't drink from it, it's to swim in."

"So let's swim in it," he suggested. It had been awhile since they had a bath, he could stand to wash some of the grime off.

"Daddy installed the pool in 1988, we might actually be home." She was trying not to get her hopes up but she couldn't help it.

"Let's check the house." Kayla led the way but her hopes were doused when she realized that they weren't in 2007 because if they were they would have seen flowerbeds under the windows—there were none.

"We haven't made it yet," she told him with her shoulders slumped.

"You're kidding me, right?"

"No."

Kin walked up to a window and peeked in, there he saw a younger version of the woman he loved, she slept peacefully, he just stared.

"What do you see?"

"I see you."

"Well, what am I doing?"

"You're sleeping."

Curiosity had gotten the best of her, she stood up beside him and looked in the window. It was her, of course she was years younger.

"I can't believe I was ever that thin."

"You're still thin."

"Not that thin," she argued.

"You were still a child then, now you're a beautiful young woman with beautiful curves." He ran his hand down her back and over her round bottom.

Kayla looked back into the window. "Oh my God."

"What is it?"

"I think I'm disappearing."

Kin looked back into the window and it looked as if the woman he loved was starting to fade.

"What's happening?" she asked.

"I don't think you're supposed to be here, I don't think you can share the same space with yourself."

"What are you saying?"

"Hell, I don't know what I'm talking about, I don't know the rules of time travel but something isn't right and I think we need to leave now."

"Before I disappear for good?"

"I guess it could happen." Kin grabbed her arm and they ran as fast as they could to the hill, to the rock, to where the rock was supposed to be.

"Where's the rock?" he yelled.

"Good question." They looked all around the area but didn't see it. Kayla found herself getting tired, she was out of breath for no reason.

"Something is wrong, Kin, what's happening to me?"

"I don't know, but we have to find that rock fast."

"I'm too tired." Kayla sat down and went limp.

"Don't you dare go to sleep on me," he warned her. He slapped her lightly on the cheek, trying to keep her alert. He looked around one more time... Finally he spotted the rock, it had been moved and was hiding behind a stump. He picked Kayla up in his arms and carried her to the rock , he jumped.

TWELVE

January 2007

"What's all of this?" Jake asked walking into the kitchen.

"It's Kayla's birthday." There were balloons tacked up on the walls and a chocolate cake sitting on the counter.

"Shelly, she has been gone for five months now, what makes you think she will be here just because it's her birthday?"

"I don't know that she will be here, but I woke up today feeling her presence, it's going to be a good day," she insisted.

"We have searched for months and nothing, now you think she's just going to walk in as if she's never been gone?"

"Why are you giving me that look, Jake?"

"What look?"

"Like I'm crazy."

"Maybe you are."

She slapped at him. It was fun to be able to joke with each other again after so many months of thinking he'd had something to do with Kayla's being gone.

"Your friend Matt keeps running his mouth about you selling the ranch to him."

"He should keep his mouth shut, I won't sell it to him." The mood turned serious again.

"So you are thinking about selling it?" She stopped what she was doing to look at him.

"I've done nothing but think about it since the day you told me she left the ranch to me, I'd be pleased as punch if she had just left it to you."

"But she didn't, she left it to you because she knows that you love it here and she wanted you to have it for your own... It doesn't matter now, she is coming home soon."

"I'm putting the finishing touches on my house, I'll be moving in soon," he said.

Shelly sat down. The past five months had been so lonely for her without Kayla. She was four months pregnant and Kayla had not been there to share it with her, she would be so happy for her.

"Don't cry, Shelly, it can't be good for the baby. Do you want me to call Bobby?"

"No, he's at work, I don't want to bother him."

"I loved her too, Shelly, I miss her but I don't think she's coming home."

"I won't believe she's dead, unless they find her body and prove without a doubt she's gone, I won't believe it."

Jake stood up and pushed his chair in, they had this conversation many times, there was no point in having it again, he turned back and looked into Shelly's sad, hollow eyes. "You need to take care of yourself and that child growing inside of you now."

"I will... Please don't sell the land to Matt, I don't like him and I don't trust him."

"I can't make any promises."

"I understand."

Kin shook his fragile woman. "Wake up, honey," he pleaded.

"What happened?"

"I'm not sure, are you okay?"

"I feel fine, why are you hovering over me?"

"Never mind, let's find out where we are."

Kayla took in the familiar surroundings. "We're home," she said with certainty.

"How can you be sure?"

"This is my barn, the way it was when I left that is." She walked over to the stall and put her hand on Jake's best horse. "This is Patty."

"So we finally made it? To your time?"

"I think so, Patty is here, let's see if Jake is too."

She stopped in her tracks.

"What's wrong now?"

"What if they think I'm dead, what if I've been gone for a year or more?"

"What if it's only been a day or two weeks? Let's just find out."

They heard voices outside the barn door. Kayla pulled Kin back when she heard Matt's voice.

"That's him."

"Who?"

"That's the last voice I heard before I found myself with you… I don't know his last name but his first name is Matt, he is a new hand that Jake hired. He was threatening me for some reason." She struggled to remember what had happened. "I didn't like him much from the first time I saw him…but that day, he said I had stolen the land from him and that he was going to get it back."

"What else did he say?"

"He said that he knew I would never sell it to him, and that's why he had to get rid of me, he said Jake would sell it to him."

"How could Jake sell your land?"

"I left it to Jake in my will."

"And how did this guy know that? Did Jake tell him?"

"I don't think Jake knew about it, I never told anyone about my will, he said that Jake had his own place and didn't want mine, he said I had to die… He tried to kill me, Kin. He pushed me, I fell and hit my head and then everything went black, and you know the rest."

They listened to the men talk.

"Come on, Jake, when are you gonna sell me the land?"

"I'm not."

"It's been long enough, the bitch is dead, just sell me the damn land."

Jake hauled off and socked him square in the jaw. "Kayla was a good woman and don't you ever say a bad word about her again."

"She was a slut, I saw her throw herself at you the night before she disappeared."

"How do you know that?"

Kin looked at Kayla, was it true? Did she throw herself at this man Jake?

"You were spying on us, on her, you were the one in her flowerbeds, you were the one Shelly saw on the hill that night."

"The other men and I were checking the cattle one night, we decided to do a little window-shopping, we saw you and the slut in the living room, she dropped her clothes and begged you to take her. A real man would have done it, but you said, 'No, I want you to love me,'" he mocked. "The bitch is dead now so she won't be needin' the land, and if you don't sell it to me I'll find another way."

"You don't know what you saw that night, and now that I know how you are I will see to it that you never get your filthy hands on this land." Jake turned to walk away.

"I'm getting this land, I have it all figured out, you can either sell it to me legally or I can get it a different way, either way I'm going to win."

"What are you babbling about, man?"

"I have proof that you're responsible for Kayla's disappearance."

"I would have to be guilty for you to have proof."

"Trust me, this will make you look guilty as hell."

"No one will believe you."

"You're the one who had the most to gain from her death, as far as anyone knows you're the last to see her, I also have proof that you've been stealing money to build your own house and furnish supplies for your ranch."

Jake grabbed Matt by the collar. "You little devil, listen to me and listen good, Reed. If I ever find out that you had something to do with Kayla's disappearance I will kill you, do you understand? I'll kill you."

"I don't know where she is, really, but if I were you I'd thinking about selling off this land, to me." Matt walked off, seemingly confident in himself.

"Did you hear what he called him?" Kin asked.

"Devil?"

"No, after that, he called him Reed."

Kayla's eyes grew large. "You Don't really believe that he is related to the other Reeds, do you?"

"I sure as hell do, he has the same sneaky ways about him. When the Reeds thought they had killed me they thought they were going to get my land, but because of you I had a chance to save myself and leave a will for Doc to inherit my land."

"And your point?"

"Somehow all these years later the Reeds still think they need to have my land, it's almost unbelievable."

"If anyone should have this land it's you, Kin, this is your land."

"No, it's yours now, Kayla, we won't let Jake sell it to anyone, he can't, you're not dead."

"I'm scared Kin, Matt wants me dead and he might even try to kill me again."

"It won't happen, Kayla, I promise, I'll protect you."

"I just want to go to the house, I want to take a warm bath and sleep in my own bed."

"Let's go."

"I don't think I'm ready for them to see me just yet, can we wait till dark? They will all be gone by then."

"Whatever you want, sweetheart."

They hid out in the barn until the sun set. When Kayla thought it was safe to go to the house she opened the barn door. The air, now much cooler, gave her a slight chill.

They walked quickly and quietly. Kin suddenly pulled her back.

"What is it?"

"There is someone in the house."

"How do you know that?"

"I see a shadow, look." He pointed to the kitchen window. He was right, someone was in the house but she couldn't see who it was until they appeared directly in front of the window.

"It's Shelly, I wonder what she's doing here so late."

"Do you want to go in and see her?"

Kayla hesitated. "I'd rather wait till morning."

"What if she doesn't leave tonight?"

"She will, sooner or later, she won't stay in the house alone." No sooner than she had finished her sentence Shelly stepped out of the house and got into her car. She sat with the motor running for a few minutes and then finally she drove away.

"She seems really sad."

"I know, I hate to see her like that, she's like a sister to me." Kayla reached under a rock for the spare key to the backdoor. When she stepped inside she gasped.

"What is it?"

"It looks like it's someone's birthday." She reached down and picked up a card off the table.

Kayla, today is your birthday, you have been away for five months, it seems like forever. They say you're not coming back but I still feel that you will. Today your presence was strong, I know you're close, I hope you find your way home soon. I have been wanting to tell you that you will be an aunt soon. I really want this child to grow up knowing his or her Aunt Kayla, so wherever you are I hope you are having a good birthday.

Love, Shelly.

Her eyes filled with tears, she couldn't talk so she just handed Kin the card so that he could read it himself.

"She really misses you."

"I bet she's been here every day since I left. I should have stopped her before she went home. I've been gone for five months, Kin."

"Apparently time flies when you're time traveling."

She couldn't help but laugh at his remark.

"Happy birthday, sweetheart." He kissed her on the neck.

"Thank you."

"I don't mean to rain on the occasion but I just have to ask you something."

"What is it?"

"Reed told that Jake guy that he saw you throw yourself at him... Was that true?"

"I'm sorry to say it is," she admitted with her head down.

"But you said that there was nothing between you and your ranch hand."

"There isn't... He turned me down."

"I don't understand why he would."

"Well, because he knows that I am not in love with him."

"But he is in love with you?"

"He seems to think he is."

"If he didn't love you he would have taken you into his bed and not cared about the aftermath."

"How do you know that?"

"It's a man thing."

"You aren't angry with me after hearing that I threw myself at another man, are you?"

"No." He looked down at the floor.

"Are you sure?"

"I can't deny that it bothers me, but the fact is that this happened before I even knew you." He picked up a knife and walked closer to her.

"What are you doing?" she asked nervously.

"I'm going to eat a piece of your birthday cake...if it's all right."

"Of course it's all right." She felt silly for thinking anything else. She had been alone and paranoid for too long. "I'm going to run us a warm bath."

"You want to bathe together?"

"Are you tired of me already?" she asked him.

"Just plain tired, honey."

"Come upstairs when you finish your cake."

Kayla stood in front of the mirror. It seemed like only a day or so since she had stood in that same spot and watched herself prepare for an evening of lust with Jake—now she prepared for an evening of love with Kin. She wiped the steam from the mirror and looked at herself again. Was it just her imagination or did she look older? Of course she was older, it was her birthday. She ran a finger along the fine lines under her eyes.

"You'll feel better after a hot bath."

Kayla jumped at the sound of his voice. "You scared me."

"I didn't mean to, what were you thinking about?"

"Everything, what if I wake up in the morning and you're gone?"

He went to her and held her tightly. "I'm not a dream, I'm real and I won't leave you... I think your water is about to spill over."

She ran to the tub and shut the water off, letting some escape out of the drain.

They undressed each other. Kin slid down into the tub and Kayla sank down between his legs. He washed her back and then she turned around and he gently washed her breasts.

"You have the most beautiful breasts," he told her as he lathered the soap. Her nipples tightened, her throat went dry, he rinsed the soap from her body and put his mouth over one hardened nipple and suckled it gently. She thought that this was the type of lovemaking that was worth waiting for, this man had been worth waiting for. She let her hand fall in the water and found his manhood at full attention, she stroked for only a second before she found herself being pulled on top of him.

"I love you so much, Kayla," he said breathlessly.

"I love you too," she told him and she meant it with all of her heart. They rocked as one, holding each other tightly until they climaxed as always…together.

They left the tub and dried each other off, she led him to her bed, pulled the covers back and they both slid between the satin sheets.

"This is nice," he told her.

"I'm glad you like it, I hope you'll stay awhile."

"I have no plans to leave you, Kayla." At that she was fast asleep in his arms.

They slept long and sound. Kin was the first to wake, he was very hungry; the birthday cake he'd eaten the night before hadn't lasted long. He slipped out of bed and tiptoed down the stairs, trying not to wake his new love. He rummaged through the icebox and found some bacon and eggs. He was planning to make Kayla breakfast in bed. It would have been a nice surprise to her but instead he was the one surprised.

"Who the hell are you?" asked a very angry female voice.

He turned to see Kayla's friend Shelly staring into his eyes. If looks could kill he'd be a goner. But the big stick she shook at him might hurt worse than the look.

"Calm down, Shelly."

"How do you know my name?"

"Kayla told me all about you."

"Where is she? What have you done with her? What have you done to her?"

Kin followed her eyes down to his lower body , he realized that he was still naked.

He reached for a kitchen towel and covered himself the best he could.

"You beast, where is she?" Shelly raised the baseball bat, ready to swing.

"I... She's..."

Kayla stepped out of the bedroom and stretched, she smelled bacon and headed for the kitchen.

"What smells so..." She stopped in her tracks at the sight of her friend holding a bat at her naked lover.

"Kayla!"

"Shelly!"

"What are you doing here?"

"I live here."

"I know that. I mean, where have you been? We have been worried sick about you, we thought you were dead, why haven't you called?" With all the questions that she'd asked she never once took her eye off of Kin and never released her grip on the bat.

"Shelly, stop talking for a minute and I'll tell you everything."

"Okay."

"You have to put the bat down. Kin isn't a threat to me or anyone else," she assured.

"All right, if you say so." She set the bat down and sat at the kitchen table. "I'm listening."

"I didn't leave by choice—

"I knew that, I told Jake and everyone else that you wouldn't—"

"Why don't we talk about this over breakfast, I did cook after all," Kin said.

"It looks like you've been doing more than that." She looked down at him again.

"Yes, well, if you ladies will excuse me I will get dressed before we eat."

"I laid out some clothes for you on the bed, I'm sure they will fit you."

He leaned down and kissed her on his way out the door.

"Sit down, Shelly," Kayla ordered.

"I cannot believe how you're acting. No one has seen or heard from you in months, and you're acting like you just left for a night. Where have you been?" Shelly was nervously shoving bacon in her mouth.

"Slow down on that, will you, you'll make the baby sick."

Shelly stopped and looked at her. "How do you know about the baby?"

Kayla held up the birthday card that Shelly had left on the table for her.

"Oh yeah!"

Kin had slipped back into the kitchen, dressed this time. He sat beside Kayla and put a reassuring hand on her thigh.

"The things that I'm about to tell you are going to sound crazy but I'm not crazy, Kin went through this with me."

"Kin, that's the name that is carved on that stupid rock of yours…and you thought someone was burried under it."

They looked at each other.

"Oh no… You're not about to tell me that I'm looking at the man that's supposedly buried under that rock."

Kayla nodded.

"So what, I'm looking at a ghost? And you're sleeping with a ghost?"

"He is not exactly a ghost since he never died, he's just almost a hundred years old."

"Well, he looks pretty darn good to be that old… Well endowed also, I see."

"You noticed that, did you?"

"It was kind of hard to miss."

Kin blushed, they talked about him as if he weren't even in the room, he wondered if women in his time sat around the table discussing such personal things.

"There is something you need to know. That Matt kid has been bugging Jake to sell him your ranch."

"I heard."

"What do you mean you heard? Have you talked to Jake already?"

"No."

"Then how do you know?"

"We were in the barn yesterday and we overheard Jake and Matt talking."

"You were here yesterday? And you didn't let us know?"

"It's not that easy, Shelly, a lot has happened."

"Yes, a lot has happened."

"Some men tried to kill us, Shelly, we had to hide and now we know that this Matt kid is related to the men that tried to kill Kin in his own time."

"I can't believe you're talking time travel, Kayla. How do you expect me to believe it?"

"I guess I don't, it was hard for Kin to believe too, but he knows it's real. We traveled through time, Shelly, I swear it's the truth."

Shelly looked to Kin for confirmation.

"Yes, it's a lot to take in but she's telling the truth."

"Okay, but even if I believe you no one else will, and I'm sorry to tell you this but a lawyer told Jake that as of today he is legally able to sell your land."

"But I'm alive, he can't do that."

"The court says he can and they are supposed to meet at the courthouse any minute to sign off and give Jake legal posession."

"Now what do I do?"

"I suggest we get you to the courthouse so that they can see you're alive."

The three of them loaded up into Shelly's car.

"I hate cars," Kin mumbled.

"Kin gets carsick," Kayla explained.

"You're kidding," Shelly laughed.

"I miss my horse."

"There are plenty of horses here still."

"They aren't Steel."

"What?" Shelly asked, confused.

"My horse, his name is Steel."

"Oh... You sound like you want to go home, Kin."

"I miss the simple life."

Kayla sat silent in the backseat. She knew that she would never go back in time again, she only hoped that Kin wouldn't either.

"Here we are." Shelly stopped the car in front of the courthouse steps and dropped Kin and Kayla off. "I'll park and meet you inside."

Kayla ran into the building with Kin hot on her heels. They found Jake and Matt in the front office. Kayla busted in.

"You're alive." Matt was shocked.

"Yes, Matt, does that surprise you? Since after all you tried to kill me."

Jake approached Kayla and hugged her, Kin watched with a jealous eye.

"Where have you been? Shelly and I have been worried sick."

"It's a long story. I'll tell you all of it but first I want that man arrested." She pointed at Matt. "He tried to kill me."

"And who are you? How do you fit into the picture?" Jake asked Kin.

"I found Kayla on my doorstep one day, lost and bleeding from a head wound."

"You can't sell my land to this would-be murderer, I won't allow it."

"Excuse me," the judge butted in. "Is this the woman who you all have been trying to convince me is dead?"

"This is her, sir," Jake said.

"Well, clearly she is alive so we won't be signing over any of her property. As for her claims of attemped murder, I'm calling the investigators in on this matter."

"Judge, she is crazy, I didn't try to kill her," Matt squirmed.

"Why would I make it up?"

"Why would you wait five months before reporting it if it were true?"

"I didn't have a choice, I couldn't get here."

"Were you being held against your will?" the judge asked.

"No, not exactly."

"Your Honor, the lady could not remember who she was when I found her on my doorstep much less where she lived, it took her awhile but now she remembers clearly that this man tried to kill her, all for a plot to get her land," Kin explained.

"Who the hell are you? And why are you wearing my clothes?" Jake asked him.

Kin looked to Kayla, she just shrugged. "Don't worry about who he is, you're about to sell my land to this no-good cheat."

"I held off as long as I could, Kay, we didn't think you were coming back."

"Even if I didn't I willed that land to you, I thought you loved that land."

"I do, but I have my own land and my own home now."

"Since when?"

"I bought the land months before you went missing and I started building the house two weeks before you disappeared."

"Where is this land? Were you ever going to tell me about this? Were you just going to up and quit and leave me with no one to help run the land?"

"No, I was looking for the right person to take my place."

"Where is your land?" she asked again.

"I'll tell you where it is," Matt blurted out. "It's on the west side of your property, that's where your cattle went, he was robbing you blind, lady, if anyone wanted to kill you it's him. Why don't you look into him?" he told the judge.

"Is that true, Jake?"

"It's true I have my own land next to yours but it's a lie that I ever tried to steal from you, I would never do that and I think you know it."

"I believe you, Jake." But she didn't sound very convincing.

A uniformed officer came into the room. "Miss, can you tell us what happened the day you disappeared?"

"Officer, for the longest time I couldn't remember how I got hurt but now it is crystal clear. Jake left me alone on the top of the hill that day. Strange things had been happening for weeks but this day Matt had approached me and he started ranting and raving on about how my family had stolen the ranch from his family, he said he wanted it back. I told him over my dead body, and he said that could be arranged, he said he would make it look like an accident. He pushed me to the ground, I hit my head, I remember seeing the blood and then I passed out. The next thing I knew I was in this man's home."

"And who are you, sir?" the officer asked Kin.

"Kin Parsons, I found the lady bleeding on my doorstep and I bandaged her up."

"And where do you live, sir?"

"He lives in Muskogee," Kayla butted in.

"How did you get that far away?"

"I don't know, I would assume that Matt took me to get rid of me."

"And you didn't know who you were? Is that correct?"

"Yes, until a few days ago I wasn't sure who I was, but I know who I am now and I know that this man wanted to kill me so that he could acquire my land."

"The police had pictures of you posted all over the state, in the papers, on the television. Didn't either of you see any of it?" The officer was suspicious of their story.

Kin and Kayla looked at each other.

"No, Kin doesn't own a television and we saw no papers… The point is that this man tried to kill me." She put her finger in Matt's face.

He turned red with anger. "You should be dead, you little whore," Matt yelled, slapping her finger away from him.

Kin and Jake both moved toward Matt but Kin reached him first.

"No one talks like that to the woman I love," he told Matt, grabbing him by the throat.

The officer rushed to them and pulled Kin away. "It looks like you might be safer in jail, son," he told Matt.

"You can't arrest me."

"Well, you have said enough to make me believe that there is some truth to this story, so until I can straighten this out I'm holding you. Ma'am, I will contact you in a day or so with more questions."

"Yes, sir."

Jake was at Kayla's side. "Who is this man?" he asked her.

"Kin, this is Jake." The men shook hands while sizing each other up.

"I want to thank you for taking care of Kayla while she was hurt," Jake told him.

"We took care of each other."

"What does that mean?" He wondered what exactly happened the past five months. Had he lost all chances with Kayla? Was this the man that he was losing her to?

"It means we are in love, Jake."

Yep, that was the last thing he had wanted to hear, that Kayla was in love with another man.

"I see." He looked down at his boots.

"I'm sorry," she told him.

"Why are you sorry? You have nothing to be sorry about, you're in love, you should be happy."

"I am happy, Kin makes me happy." She smiled up at him.

"That's all that matters to me, Kay. If you're happy then I am happy for you. I don't know if Kin can ranch or not—"

"I know ranching like the back of my hand," Kin interrupted.

"Then I suppose I can call off the search for someone to take over the ranch, you'll be fine without me."

"You don't have to leave the ranch, Jake."

"I have my own ranch to deal with now, Kay, and you don't need me anymore."

"I'll always need you, Jake. Aside from Shelly you're my best friend. We can still be friends, can't we?"

"We will always be friends. If you need anything, anything at all, just call me."

"I will," she promised.

At that moment Shelly ran into the room breathless.

"What happened? Did I miss everything?"

"I'm afraid the show is over."

"Did they take Matt to jail? Did he admit that he tried to kill you?"

"They took him to jail, for now at least."

"Can I give anyone a ride home?" Jake asked.

"You can take me home," Shelly said. "Kayla and Kin can take my car."

"Come on then." Jake took Shelly by the arm and ushered her out of the courthouse. He nodded as he passed Kin and Kayla.

"So how much do you know about this Kin fellow?" Jake questioned once they got on the road.

"Well, obviously I just met him this morning. He's got a nice butt," she added.

"I can't believe you've already checked him out."

"I couldn't help it, when I found him in the house this morning he was cooking Kayla breakfast…in the nude."

"Are you serious? What a bastard."

"Do you really not like the man or are you just jealous?"

"What are you talking about?"

"I know that you have been in love with Kayla for a long time."

"You don't know anything," he snapped at her.

"Kay told me about the night she threw herself at you and you turned her down."

"She would have regretted it the next day, if not sooner."

"If all you wanted was her body you would have taken it. Face it, Jake, you're a gentleman and you love her."

"I should have made love to her that night. Maybe things would be different today."

"No, you did the right thing, and you know it. Don't you?"

"I don't know... Do you think she looks happy?"

"I think she is very happy, in love. I haven't seen that light in her eyes since before her parents died."

"All that matters is she's happy. If this Kin man makes her happy then I'm fine with that." He pulled into Kayla's driveway and opened the door to let Shelly out.

"Jake, you're a wonderful man and soon a woman that deserves your love will come along and you will be happy."

"I'll be an old man before that happens."

"Will you stop that talk, I have a feeling that you'll meet that special someone very soon, and when you do you will know that she is the one."

"I hope you're right, Shelly."

"I'm always right." She kissed him on the cheek and skipped into the house like a child .

Kin and Kayla sat in the car still parked in the courthouse parking lot.

"I don't care what you say, that man is in love with you, Kayla."

"You sound like Shelly. He's not in love with me," she denied.

"I know what I saw, and that was a man in love."

"Are you jelous?" She pulled the car onto the road.

"Hell yes, I am, you have known him longer, what if you decide you want him instead of me? Will you please slow this thing down, I feel sick again."

Kayla pulled the car over and put it in park, letting the engine idle. "The only man I love is you, it isn't going to change, do you understand?"

"Are you sure?"

"I am absolutely sure," she told him.

Kayla pulled the car back onto the road and when they reached her home Jake and Shelly were standing on the porch waiting for them.

"What took you so long? Did you stop to make out?" Shelly asked.

"Shelly." Kayla rolled her eyes, it did no good to reprimand her because Shelly was who she was and said what she thought, no matter how inappropriate it might be.

"Kayla, we should talk in the office, you haven't been here for a long time and I need to explain some of the spending I did while you were away."

She looked to Kin.

"Go on, I'll be fine," he assured her.

"I'll take good care of him." Shelly winked at her friend, taking Kin's arm in hers.

"That's what I'm afraid of."

THIRTEEN

Jake had taken Kayla into her office, he showed her the receipts for everything that he had purchased while she was gone.

"So as you can see, I only spent what I had to, and payed the hands. By the way, two of them are gone."

"Why?"

"We didn't need them, your father kept them on because he felt sorry for them. They only stayed because they felt obligated to him."

"I see."

"People have been talking , saying that I've been stealing money from you all along to pay for my own rach and house, I wanted to show you that it's not true, I can account for every penny of your money I spent."

"Jake, I trust you with my life, I know you didn't steal from me."

"I loved your father like he was my own, I would never take from you to benefit myself."

"I know that, Jake, you don't have to convince me, my father had complete trust in you and so do I."

Jake took Kayla's hands in his and looked directly into her eyes.

Shelly was talking but Kin was not listening.

"Where are you going?" she asked.

"Just to get a drink of what you call tap water, I'll be right back, Shelly."

"Good, I can't wait to hear more about where you come from."

Kin wandered through the house. He hadn't really been thirsty but he was curious about what was taking Jake and Kayla so long. He approached the office. The door was slightly open. He peeked in and saw them holding hands. He started to turn away angry but instead he waited and listened.

"Kayla, you must know that I love you."

"Jake, you don't love me."

"I do and you know it, you just don't want to admit it because you don't love me back."

"Jake, I—"

"Don't say anything." He put a finger to her lips to shush her. "I can't make you love me, I wouldn't want to make you. I saw the way you looked at Kin, you're in love with him and I think he feels the same. It's okay, I want you to know that I understand, but if he ever hurts you don't think for a second that I won't kill the man."

"I don't think you have to worry about him hurting me."

"I hope not, I'd like to know more about the guy, where did he come from? I'd like to know the whole story, Kay."

"It's very long and cofusing."

"I have time."

"I'll tell you all about it someday."

"But not today?"

"No, Jake, not today."

He released her hands. "Go on then, find your man."

"Thank you, Jake."

"No problem."

She kissed him on the cheek and slipped down the hall. An arm reached out and grabbed her from the kitchen doorway, she let out a scream that was cut off by a mouth being pressed over hers. Kin searched for her tongue and found it. They shared a deep, long kiss before he released her.

"You scared me."

"I'll do it more often if it makes you kiss me like that."

"You don't have to scare me to make me kiss you like that. Why aren't you outside with Shelly?"

"I got thirsty...and my ears were starting to bleed," he joked.

"You'll get used to her, soon you'll love her as much as I do."

"If you say so. Let's take a walk."

"I have a better idea, let's go for a ride."

"Not in the car," he whined.

"No, on the horses."

"Now that I can handle," he said, relieved.

"Let's ride up the hill, I want to see something. I'll have Jake show you around the rest of the property later."

"Are you forgetting that I used to own this land?"

"No, but it has changed a little bit, and if you're going to be running it you should know how things work these days."

"What about Jake?"

"He is leaving, he has his own ranch to run now and if you don't want to work it then I will have to do it myself."

"We wouldn't want that now, would we?"

"I would rather spend the time in my flowerbeds, and maybe learn to cook a little better."

"You don't have to do that for me."

"I want to do it for you, I want to do everything for you, Kin."

"Stop here." He helped Kayla off her horse and they stepped up to the tree where the initials were carved.

"This tree is still here after all this time," he said.

"I wish it weren't."

"Why?"

"Because it is just a reminder that you loved someone else before me."

"Don't think like that now; it's you and me forever, sweetheart."

"I know it's silly, but I can't help the way that I feel." Kayla looked down at her feet and her gaze followed a small trail that led straight to the rock.

"Kin, look, the rock is still here."

"My name is still on it."

"Shouldn't it have disappeared?"

"I don't know, I haven't read the rule book on time travel."

"Do you think it means something?"

"Maybe we aren't finished yet," he stated.

"I'm finished, I don't want to go through time anymore." Kayla rubbed her hands together as if to wash her hands from the whole situation.

"What if I am supposed to go back?"

"You can't leave me, Kin, I love you and I want you to stay with me forever."

"What if it isn't up to me?" He bent down to move the rock.

"Don't," she pleaded, trying to pull him away from the rock, but he pushed her aside and rolled the rock over. She closed her eyes.

"It's green, Kayla, it's green." He shook his head back and forth.

"I don't care, I won't let you go back, they will kill you for sure."

"What if I have to go? What if there's someone who needs my help?"

"I don't care, I won't let you go back, I won't let you." She clung to him.

"I have to see what's going on, Kayla."

"I just found you, I don't think I can live with out you." Tears blocked her vision.

"I promise to love you forever, Kayla. I will never leave you."

"I just want to go to the house and make love to you," she told him, planting kisses all about his face. They rode the horses to the barn and a ranch hand put them up for the night. They made their way into the house. Kin picked her up and carried her into the bedroom. Kicking the door shut behind them, he pulled his shirt off and with one swift move he pulled her dress up over her head and tossed it over his shoulder. They made passionate love all night long as if they would never see each other again.

Kin awoke before sunup. He had an uneasy feeling. He crept down the stairs to the fire place. The air had a chill to it so he started a fire. He looked at the family pictures on the mantle; Kayla and her parents smiled in every portrait. He just couldn't seem to shake the uneasy feeling he had.

"What are you doing out of bed?"

Kin jumped at the sound of her voice, maybe it was the ice-cold touch of her hands.

"I thought I'd start a fire, your hands are so cold." He took her hands in his and tried to warm them. Are you feeling all right, Kayla?"

"I'm fine, just a little tired."

"Is that all?"

"We made love five times last night, I think I've earned the right to be tired."

Kin swept her up in his arms again and carried her back to bed. "You did earn that right, that's why you're going back to bed." Kin carefully put her back into bed and in minutes she was fast asleep. He watched her carefully, she appeared paler than usual. He returned to the mantle and the family pictures. His eyes were focused on Kayla's image, it seemed to be fading.

"What's so interesting?"

"Oh, morning, Shelly."

"Where's Kay?" She tossed her coat on the sofa.

"She's asleep, she's not feeling well this morning."

"I'm sorry to hear that, we were going to go shopping this morning."

"These pictures are faded," he said, not particularly to her.

"Pictures do that as they age."

"No, not like this."

"What are you talking about, Kin?"

"This morning, not an hour ago, this picture was normal, and now it's fading, Kayla's image is fading."

Shelly stood by his side. She did think the picture looked a little faded but he was really taking it hard.

"Is there something I should know about, Kin?"

"I have to go outside, I'll be right back."

It was no use trying to stop him, the man was clearly on a mission. He ran to the top of the hill and rolled the rock over again, he stared at the green fog, he began to see images in it, he saw two men, they were fighting, soon he saw Doc clear as day, he was in the argument now. One man rode off, leaving Doc looking up into the the sky yelling something. Suddenly Kin's name rang out. Doc was calling for him, something was wrong, terribly wrong. He had to get back to his time to help Doc, not only Doc but Kayla—this had something to so with why her image was fading, he was sure of it.

He ran back through the door. "Is Kayla awake yet?"

"No, I just checked on her, she's sound asleep, what's wrong?"

Kin took Shelly by her shoulders. With a deadly serious face he told her that he had to go back.

"Back where?"

"In time."

"No, you can't leave, I won't let you leave her."

"I have to, trust me, I'll be back as soon as possible."

"You should tell her yourself."

Kin showed her the picture again.

"It looks more faded than it did just a few minutes ago."

"I know, I'm afraid that if I don't get back in time Kayla might not ever exist."

Shelly put her hands on either side of her head. "Oh! This is more than I can handle, I can't believe this is happening."

"But it is happening." He looked up at the staircase. "I'll be back, I promise."

Kin ran out the front door and it slammed behind him.

Kayla woke up at the sound of the door slam. She ran quickly down to the living room.

"What's all the racket down here?"

"Nothing."

"I know when you're lying, Shelly, where is Kin?"

"I don't know."

"Where is he?" she asked again.

"I think you should sit down for this."

Kayla dropped the coffee cup that she had been holding; it shattered on the floor.

"I can't let him go, Shelly." She ran out the door with Shelly following close behind. She knelt at the rock, there was no familiar green glow, no way for her to go back to the past, and in her mind no way for Kin to return to the future.

"Did he say anything at all to you, Shelly?"

"He said he didn't want to leave but he had to go and that he promised he would come back to you, I don't remember all of it, he rambled a lot but he showed me the photo on your mantle and your image was beginning to fade."

"What?"

"I swear, Kay, he didn't want to leave but he felt he had to, he promised he would come back and I believe that he will."

"What am I going to do without him?"

"The same thing you did before him, you'll manage."

"What if he can't come back?"

"I saw the look in his eyes, Kay, he will come back, or die trying."

"That's what I'm afraid of."

FOURTEEN

Kin spiraled through time once again. Landing hard on the hard ground in a puff of dust, he found himself lying at someone's feet. When he looked up he smiled and laughed.

"Doc, you old goat, how ya been?" He stood up and gave the old man a pat on the back.

"It's good to see you again, son."

"It's good to see you too, but I was hopin' not to have to come back."

"How's the girl?"

"Doc, something isn't right, we finally made it back to her home and we should be starting our life together but instead I've been called back here.Why did you call my name, Doc, what's wrong?"

"How on earth did you know I was calling for you?"

"I just did." He looked over, just realizing that there was another man standing there, listening to every word they said. Kin sized him up.

"Kin, this is my son, Jimmy."

"Nice to meet you, Jimmy." Kin shook his hand.

"I heard you was dead."

"Well…that's a long story I'd rather not get into right now. What's going on, Doc?"

"Kin, walk with me to the cabin."

There was a new cabin built on his land now in the same spot that the other had burnt down and there were small children running around.

"Who do these rascals belong to?" he asked.

"These are my grandkids, I finally convinced my boy to come home."

"Good, I'm glad to see this place is being taken care of, of course I knew it would be because it's still going strong in the future."

"What's the future like, Kin?"

"You wouldn't believe me if I told you, I don't think you would like it, Doc."

"But you like it?"

"It's not that I like the future so much, but it's who is waiting for me there. I can't live without her, Doc, your great-great-granddaughter is the woman I want to marry."

"Who?"

"Kayla, it turns out she is your great-great-granddaughter."

"You ain't foolin me, are you, son?"

"I wouldn't do that to you, Doc."

"No wonder I felt a connection of some sort to the filly. Hot damn, I met my great-great-granddaughter." Doc walked in circles, trying to wrap his mind around this news, it was like a dream.

"You'll be happy to know that Kayla still owns this land and we plan on running it together—if I can get back to her."

"Why did you come back, son?"

"I don't know yet, tell me what's happening with the Reeds."

"The same ol' threats, they want us to leave the land, just hand it over or they will kill us like they did you."

"I'm going to settle this once and for all. Give me your gun, Doc."

"You can't be serious, you're supposed to be dead, you can't just go riding in on your horse and face them. They will shoot you again."

"Speaking of horse, where is Steel? I've missed the ol' boy."

"He's in the barn, he's not as fast as he was when you left."

"Why? Did he get hurt?"

"It's been three years since you left, son, he's just getting older."

"Three years? It's only been days."

"Not here, son."

"I need that gun, Doc, Kayla's life depends on it."

"I'll get it, meet me in the barn."

Kin ran to the barn. When he opened the door none of the animals paid him any mind.

He whistled the familiar whistle that always got Steel's attention. The big animal moved to the stall door and ran his big nose across Kin's cheek, and his big tongue over his face.

"It's nice to know that I was missed. But you know how I feel about that tongue, keep it to yourself… We have a job to do, boy, I need you to be fast, and if at all possible I'll take you back with me this time."

"Just what are you planning to do, son?"

Kin jumped at the sound of Doc's voice behind him.

"Doc, you gotta stop sneaking up on people."

"I wasn't sneaking, you just weren't paying attention, you was too busy kissin' on that horse."

"I was not."

"Sure, now what have you got planned for the Reeds?"

"I don't really have a plan yet."

"Well, it's getting dark and you can't do much in the dark so you might as well come in for supper."

There was no point in arguing. Doc was right, there was nothing he could do until daylight. He followed Doc into the cabin and met all of the people inside. They had made his land their own and he almost felt uncomfortable on his own property. It didn't make any difference now soon he and Kayla would be making a family and he would have his home again. The group ate and talked and had a good time getting to know each other but through it all Kin could not stop thinking about Kayla and how she might be doing. Was she ill, was she dead, had something changed the future by him coming back to the past? He had to get back to her soon.

"Excuse me all. Thank you so much for a lovely meal and great conversation but I think I'll turn in for the night, I'll just make me a pallet in the barn."

"We can make room in the cabin," Doc offered.

"No, the barn will be just fine," he insisted.

"Good night, Mr. Parsons," the kids rang out in unison.

"Good night, all, sleep well."

Kin made his way to the barn and made himself a bed for the night. If he were lucky he would be back in bed with Kayla by the next evening; he wished she were in his arms right now. He tossed and turned most of the night and just as he was about to drift off he heard a noise outside, voices. He'd know those voices anywhere, they belonged to the Reeds. He listened as they planned an ambush on Doc and his family. They had the cabin surrounded. There were three of them and one of him, it always seemed to work out that way. If the other men hadn't been in the cabin sound asleep he would have more help but it look as if he were on his own.

He checked his gun—four bullets. Not bad but not good either. He searched the barn and found a knife, it was good and sharp. He let Steel out of the stall, he knew he would come to his rescue if need be; however, he hoped it wouldn't be necessary.

"Stay put, boy, unless I call for you," he told his horse.

He stepped out of the barn. He saw Pete in front of the cabin, he couldn't see the other men at this point.

"Looks like it's you first, Pete," he said to himself. He picked up a rock and tossed it at the man's feet. Pete bent down to pick up the rock and when he stood back up he was face to face with Kin.

"Who the hell are you?" he asked Kin.

"Don't you remember me, Pete? You should, after all you did try to kill me."

"I did kill you, yer dead, I can't be talkin' to a dead man."

"No, dead men don't talk, and soon you will join the dead." With that said Kin took the knife from its sheath and stabbed Pete in the chest as he was still falling to the ground

Kin was already in search of the next Reed man. He crept up behind Teddy.

"Boo!"

"What the hell?" Teddy turned around with his gun pointed at Kin.

"I'm back."

"Are you a ghost?" he asked.

"Do I look like a ghost?"

"No." Teddy put out his hand to touch Kin just to see if he was real. He quickly ran for cover to where Pete had been and now his brother Bob was there also, bending over the dead body of his brother.

"Run for it, Bob, Parsons is alive."

"He killed Pete," Bob told Teddy as he pulled his simple-headed brother behind some barrels for cover. They loaded their gun and took aim on Kin. They fired shot after shot but they never hit him. Teddy made a run for the horses but Kin couldn't take a shot without leaving his cover. Soon the shootout started again but Kin was not shooting. He stayed still until the night was quiet again. When he stood up to look around he saw all three Reed men, dead. Doc and his son Jimmy were standing on the porch with guns still smoking.

"How can we thank you, Kin? If you hadn't come back we might all be dead."

"I should be thanking you, Doc, I was in a heap of trouble

before you and Jim came out. I guess we helped each other, this must be why I had to come back."

"I'm glad that you did, son, I wish you could stay but I know you must go back."

"Back to where? I'm still confused," Jim said.

"Don't worry about it, son, just know that this man has went through a lot to come back and help us get rid of the Reeds."

"I did it as much for myself as for you."

"Nothin' wrong with that, son, nothin' at all."

"I'd like to take Steel with me this time."

"Sure, he's been worthless without you anyway."

"Good-bye, Doc, Jimmy."

"Good-bye, Kin." They shook hands for what would be the last time and Kin rode up to the hill. He breathed a sigh of relief; he was sure that he would be holding Kayla in his arms soon.

When he reached the top he saw Kelly Hall Wilson standing over the rock, she was sobbing. Should he let her see him, he wondered.

FIFTEEN

Kayla had been in bed for five months, she took ill when Kin left and three weeks later the doctor gave her the news that she was with child. She cried for three days straight, she was so happy to be carrying the child of the man she loved; however, she wondered if he would ever return to be with them. The doctor could not find an answer as to why Kayla was so weak. He instructed a nurse to stay with her and for Kayla to stay on bed rest. But today Kayla woke up full of energy and she could not stay in bed any longer. She asked the nurse to go up to the attic and bring down some boxes, once in a while she would see her mother looking through two red boxes and when she was done they were put back in the attic. She never knew what was in them and she never asked, but now she was ready to know what her mother found so interesting in those boxes.

Nurse Jean brought down the boxes and set them in front of Kayla. She pulled off the lid of the smaller box and found pictures, old photos that she had never seen before.

"Kayla, what are you doing?"

"Oh, Shelly, I had Jean bring these down, remember Mom would bring these down every so often to look at them, I think it's time I saw what they are."

Shelly sat down beside her friend.

"Where's the baby?"

"He's asleep on the guest bed… Who is this?" she asked, pulling a picture from the stack.

It was a little boy with curly red hair. Kayla took it out of her hand and ran her finger across the boy's image. She turned it over and read her brother's name out loud.

"*Tyler Price*… My brother."

"I didn't know that you had a brother."

"I didn't either until recently, I met him during our travel through time."

"What?"

"I actually got to meet my brother, he was three. And I got to see my parents again."

"I'm still having a hard time wrapping my mind around the fact that you traveled through time, I want to do it."

"Trust me, Shelly, it's not all good."

"But you got to see your brother you didn't know you had. They never told you about him?"

"No."

"Do you know what happened to him?"

"I think it was cancer, he was already very sick at three." Kayla rummaged through the box some more and came across a letter with her name on it, it was in her mother's handwriting.

"Can you read it to me, Shelly?"

"Sure." She took the pink stationairy out of her friend's hand.

Dearest Kayla,

I'm sure you will find this soon after your father and I are gone. This is a picture of your older brother, Tyler. He was born in 1963, we loved him as much as we loved you. We never told you about him, I don't know why, perhaps we should have, maybe it was selfish of us to keep him from you but it was hard to talk about our sweet boy after he left us. He had terminal cancer, he died shortly after you were born. He was so happy when we brought home his little sister, he couldn't wait to help take care of you;

however, the Lord must have needed him more in Heaven.

When you started school and were gone most of the day I started sitting up in the attic talking to Tyler, sometimes I actually thought he would talk back, your father thought I was crazy at times, but I know that he could hear my every word. I wanted to tell you so many times about your wonderful brother but I just never could. This box will tell you a lot about him in his short lifetime. I hope you can forgive us for keeping this huge secret for so long. Your father and I love you very much.

Love, Mom.

"Wow! Are you all right?"

Kayla bowed her head and sobbed; it seemed like that was all she did since Kin had left.

She sobbed for him and now she sobbed for the little boy she met briefly, for the older brother who was taken from her family way too soon.

She pulled another photo from the box and laughed.

"What is it?"

She showed Shelly the photo of Tyler wearing the necklace that she had given him on his third birthday in 1966.

"It's your necklace, how did it get in that picture? I thought your Dad gave that to you on your sixteenth birthday."

"He did, but I gave it to Tyler on his third birthday, I remember his face when I gave it to him, he said this is for a girl, but then he said he would wear it proudly because I gave it to him."

"That's freaky."

"Yeah, sort of, but now I know why we ended up in 1966... So I would have the chance to meet my brother."

"It must have been incredible."

"It was... Well, it wasn't all fun, we did land in jail and we had to steal food; we were chased by the police in every year we stopped in ."

"And so when did you have time to make a baby?"

"That had to have happened after we got home," she said, rubbing her tummy.

"Kin will be so excited."

"If he ever finds out. Oh, Shelly, I'm so afraid he won't make it back to us."

"He will come back."

"You sound so sure of it."

"I am. I stopped by the fire mantle on the way up and look at this." She showed Kayla the picture of her and her father that had appeared faded months ago when Kin left, but now it was like brand new again.

"That's weird."

"Yes, and I noticed that you seem to be feeling better."

"I do, I feel incredible today."

"Whatever the reason Kin had to go back it seems to have helped you."

"I do feel better."

"Do you want to call the doctor and get checked out?"

"No, but I would like to go for a walk."

"Do you think that's a good idea?"

"If you go with me I'll be fine."

"I guess your nurse might be willing to watch BJ for us, you'd better put on a sweater, there is a chill in the air."

Kin stood only feet away from his door to the future, his door back to Kayla. But Kelly was blocking his path, she stood just staring at the rock, she had the oddest expression on her face, as if she might actually be able to see the green fog that so far only he and Kayla had been able to see. She started to turn around, sensing that some one was behind her.

"You are alive," she said.

"Yes, I'm alive."

Kelly ran into his arms she kissed him full on the lips but Kin did not kiss her back. Before Kayla had come into his life he wanted nothing more than Kelly to come back to him but now Kayla was his life. He had nothing left for Kelly but pity.

"How did you survive?"

"It wasn't easy, what are you doing here, Kelly?"

"Doc put your name on this rock when he thought you were dead."

"I know."

"Why didn't you tell me you were really alive?"

"I couldn't, I could tell no one or I would have really been killed."

"The Reeds?" she asked.

"Yes, but they won't ever hurt anyone ever again."

Kelly bowed her head and started to cry. "Kin, I've missed you so much, leaving you was the biggest mistake I ever made. I can't believe I ever left you to marry that terrible man."

"I begged you not to go, you made your choice."

"It was a bad choice." She put her arms around him once more. "I'll go with you now, it can be like before, I'll be a good wife to you, I will."

Kin pushed her away. "It's too late, Kelly, I have a wonderful woman that's waiting for me to return to her and she loves me."

"Who? Who is she?"

"You don't know her."

"She could never love you like I do."

"You loved me so much that you left me for a man you didn't love , you wanted his money. Kayla would never do that."

With that said Kin mounted his horse and rode for the green fog. Together man and horse vanished, leaving Kelly alone and distraught.

Kayla and Shelly had taken their walk, Kayla was still in her nightgown but she had a sweater wrapped around her shoulders to fight off the little chill, she sat down on the porch in the rocker that her father had loved so much while Shelly went in to check on her child.

She closed her eyes and relaxed but it was short lived because she heard what sounded like a tree being chopped down. She walked to the edge of the porch and looked around, one of the horses was out. She looked closer, it wasn't just any horse—it was Steel.

Her heart jumped, she ran to the bottom of the hill, where the horse met her. She climbed on his back, taking twice as long considering her protruding belly. Steel took her up the hill and led her to the tree that had shared Kin and Kellys initials, the symbol of the love they had once shared long ago. The tree was no longer standing. Kin was now carving something else into the tree next to it. Kayla looked over his shoulder to read, it said *Kin loves Kayla for all eternity*. Tears welled up in her eyes.

"I was beginning to think you weren't coming back," she said.

He turned to look at her, his face lighting up at the sight of her.

"How are you feeling?" he asked, going to her side.

"I feel great now that you're home… You are home, aren't you?"

"I am, and I'm never leaving you again."

"Is that a promise?"

"Oh yes."

"Will you help me off this horse, please," she asked, reaching out to him.

Kin took his love by the hand and helped her off the horse. He noticed she felt a little heavier. She looked to be with child.

"Just how long have I been gone?"

"Too long, but you were here long enough to make a baby before you left."

"Thank God it's mine."

"Did you think I would find someone else when you left me?"

"About that, I had to go. The Reeds were going to kill Doc and his family, and you wouldn't exist if that happened, I had to stop them."

"Did you?"

"We did, all three of them are dead. Too bad we didn't stop the whole line of Reeds."

"I know, but if it weren't for Matt we might not be together now. He's in jail for a long time by the way."

"That's good to know."

"All that matters now is that we are together, and soon we will have a son."

"How do you know it's a boy?"

"Miracles of modern medicine." They walked hand in hand down the hill towards their home.

"I was thinking, Kin… Could we name him Tyler?"

Kin thought for a brief moment.

"Tyler Parsons… I think that would be fine, just fine…

About the Author:

I was born and raised in Delano, California. In 1994 my husband and I moved along with our daughter Aimee to McAlester, Oklahoma. For four years I ran a bookstore and even though I always loved to read, it was during these years that my love for writing began. I hope you have as much fun reading *Bed of Roses* as I did writing it.

CPSIA information can be obtained at www.ICGtesting.com
Printed in the USA
LVOW06s0858210813

348845LV00003B/218/P